Murder at Farrington Hall

Book 1

A Dodo Dorchester Mystery
by
Ann Sutton

©2020 Ann Sutton

No part of this book may be reproduced in any form whatsoever, whether by graphic, visual, electronic, film, microfilm, tape recording or any other means, without the prior written permission of the author and publisher, except in case of brief critical reviews.

This is a work of fiction. The characters, names, incidents, places and dialogue are products of the author's imagination and are not to be construed as real. The opinions and views expressed herein belong solely to the author.

Permission for the use of sources, graphics and photos is the responsibility of the author.

Published by

Wild Poppy Publishing LLC
Highland, UT 84003

Distributed by Wild Poppy Publishing

Cover design by Julie Matern
Cover Design ©2020 Wild Poppy Publishing LLC

Edited by Jolene Perry

For Armand Matern

List of Characters

The Dorchesters

Lady Dorothea "Dodo" Dorchester	Amateur sleuth and fashion icon
Lady Diantha "Didi" Dorchester	Dodo's younger sister
Lady Guinevere Dorchester	Dodo's mother
Lord Alfred Dorchester	Dodo's father, Earl of Trowbridge

The Farringtons

Freddy Farrington	Childhood friend of Dodo
Octavia "Tavie" Farrington	Hostess for the weekend, mother of Freddy
Richard Farrington	Father of Freddy

Other guests of the Farringtons

Julian Jeffries	Friend of Freddy
Charlie Chadwick	Friend of Freddy and Dodo
Marcus Makepeace	Friend of Freddy
Anita Anderson	Neighbor of Freddy
Anne and Arthur Alexander	Old friends of the Farringtons

Servants

Agnes Brown	Lady's maid of the Farringtons
Maisie Briggs	Maid
Mrs. McCreddy	Farrington's housekeeper

Policemen

Inspector Hornby	Local detective
Chief Inspector Blood	Scotland Yard detective

Table of Contents

Chapter 1 1
Chapter 2 8
Chapter 3 17
Chapter 4 24
Chapter 5 31
Chapter 6 39
Chapter 7 44
Chapter 8 54
Chapter 9 59
Chapter 10 64
Chapter 11 70
Chapter 12 78
Chapter 13 88
Chapter 14 97
Chapter 15 107
Chapter 16 112
Chapter 17 120
Chapter 18 127
Chapter 19 132
Chapter 20 138
Chapter 21 147
Chapter 22 158
About the Author 164

Chapter 1

London, England 1923
Dodo

As yet another slender, young woman sashayed along the catwalk in a dress that was positively ghastly, the Honorable Lady Dorothea Dorchester stifled a yawn. She glanced at her dainty gold watch. Would it be rude to leave mid-show?

As a well-respected patron of fashion, Dodo had been invited to this young designer's display. She had only accepted as a favor to her mother, the young couturier being the daughter of a friend. She knew that her attendance could boost the fledgling fashion house's profile, putting them on the fashion map more effectively than any amount of marketing in the press would do. She closed her eyes and breathed in deeply. No, she must not leave. Her departure would be interpreted as disfavor and that would negate the very help she hoped to give.

Dodo scooped her glossy, black hair behind her diamond-studded ear, folded her gloved hands carefully over her aristocratic knees, and plastered a smile on her beautiful face just as an enthusiastic photographer leaned forward and snapped a picture of her. *That was close!* A huge picture of Lady Dorothea Dorchester yawning, splashed all over the papers, would have been disastrous!

Resigned to her fate, she dragged a scarlet fingernail down the program to see what she could expect next. Tennis wear. Could they be more predictable? The French were so much more creative in their designs.

As a long, pleated, tennis skirt flounced by, she felt another yawn coming and looked around for more stealthy cameramen. As she checked, she was thrilled to see a familiar, feminine figure bounding toward her, a genial expression of excitement radiating from her fair face. *Saved!*

The pretty, young girl shimmied along the row, begging pardon and spilling apologies as she tripped and stumbled, stepping clumsily on several ladies' feet.

Flopping into the chair next to her sister, Diantha Dorchester gasped, "Golly, that was a lot more difficult than it should have been!"

"Didi, you didn't tell me you were coming!" smiled Dorothea, wrapping her younger sister in a big hug. "You have saved me from dying of boredom!" she said, sotto voce.

"Oh, is it that bad?" Didi replied, her golden curls bouncing as she settled into her chair.

"It is so utterly predictable!" Dorothea exclaimed. "It doesn't help that I was in Paris last week and was quite transported by *their* new styles. This just doesn't compare."

"Do you want to leave, then?" The expression on her younger sister's face was equal parts frustration at the possibility that her struggle had been in vain, and a desire to please her beloved sister.

"No, no," Dodo assured her, "I'm here as a favor. If I leave, it will spoil everything for the designer. Though I *am* going to make some helpful suggestions."

A ghastly gown in fuchsia chiffon was floating down the stage and Dorothea groaned.

"Here," announced Didi, as she leaned down to retrieve something from her capacious purse, "this will cheer you up, Dodo!" She flourished a thick, linen card, embossed with gold leaf in front of her sister's face.

Dorothea turned sharply, her fashionable bob swinging like velvet opera curtains.

"It's an invitation to Farrington Hall for a long weekend!" burst out Didi. "I haven't seen darling Freddy in ages—I think it was at Rowena Cuthbert's coming out that I last saw him!"

"How marvelous!" said Dorothea, her enthusiasm matching her sister's. She snatched the gilded invitation from Didi's fingers and read,

You are hereby invited to a party weekend at
Farrington Hall.
There will be croquet, music, dancing, and lots of laughs.

"Isn't it fabulous?" declared Didi. "It arrived this morning before I got up. Do you think Daddy will let us use the Bentley, Dodo?"

Dorothea had recently learned to drive and was eager to practice at every opportunity, but her old-fashioned father was less enthusiastic about women behind the wheel.

"I think we'll have to wait for just the right moment to ambush him with that inquiry." She laughed behind her hand.

"I wonder who else will be there?" mused Didi. "It will be my first party since coming home from finishing school in Switzerland. What fun we will have in the evenings! Do you think they have a gramophone? We could take some of our latest recordings." Her words were cascading out as they always did when she was excited. It was so good to have her back. Her sister was only two years younger, and she had missed her terribly.

"Remember, you are not the host, darling. Octavia will have plenty of recordings, I'm sure. Her exalted reputation as a hostess is well-deserved, as you know!"

"I do know! I trust they've invited some interesting chaps—oh, sorry that was tactless of me!" Didi apologized.

"It's fine. I'm over him. It took some time I admit, but I am not languishing away my youth yearning after that—that good for nothing!" she declared. "No, I feel quite disposed to jump back into the pond. My heart is a freshly blank slate."

"I'm very glad to hear it," said Didi, leaning her head closer. "You're much too pretty to be a bystander in the game of romance, and I for one am very eager about joining in. I long for some intrigue! There were far too few males near that stuffy finishing school. We were all so desperate, we would get dewy-eyed over the janitor, for goodness sake! He was thirty if he was a day!"

Dodo threw back her silky head and laughed just as a rather ghastly pair of slacks slithered along the catwalk. She prayed that her laughter would not be mistaken for ridicule, though in truth the trousers were pretty awful and deserved it. She quickly rearranged her features.

"Did you have anyone in mind?" Didi pursued.

"Well, not Freddy!" Dodo chuckled. "Sweet though he is, he's more the brotherly sort and anyway, he's rather too short for me. No, I'm as interested to see who else is invited as you are."

A stick-thin model in a gold lamé dress tiptoed down the stage in perilously high heels, holding a masquerade mask to her gaunt features. Both the sisters stopped talking and gawped. This was a new low. Dodo fought the urge to frown.

Mercifully, the golden horror was the final gown of the show, and next, all the models would gather as the designer came out to receive her accolades. Dodo pinched her lips, making a pretense at applauding, then quickly rose to make her exit before the crowds.

"Come on! Let's get out of here!" she hissed at her sister.

They stumbled back along the row and high-tailed it for the doors like shipwrecked sailors lunging toward a rescue ship.

A flash blinded them both and they stopped short, hands protecting their faces, as the doors swung to behind them.

"Lady Dorothea, what did you think of the new autumn line?" A journalist had successfully ambushed them, and Dodo's eyes were smarting from the bright light. *Irritating.*

"I endeavor to support young designers when I can," she began carefully. "The Great War devastated the fashion industry. It is still recovering. I believe that England can and should take its rightful place in the world of couture if given the right encouragement and support. Thank you."

She pushed her sister forward and they both bolted, leaving the journalist to bellow, "But you didn't answer my question!"

"Taxi!" Dodo cried, stepping out onto the street in front of a sleek, black cab that stopped abruptly. She yanked open the door and thrust her sister in, falling awkwardly behind her. "Victoria Station!" she barked at the driver.

"Phew! That was close!" Dodo said, pulling off her gloves and scarf and looking out the back window to see the newsman rushing out to the pavement. "It's so hard to be honest in those situations without damaging reputations and careers. I do hate it when they lay in wait for one like that!"

"I suppose it's jolly awkward for you," agreed Didi. "One wrong word from the Honorable Lady Dorothea Dorchester and the unfortunate thing's dreams would go up in smoke!"

"Yes, but those designs *were* extraordinarily frightful! Not condemning them may hurt my *own* reputation!" They both giggled. "Perhaps I can help by introducing her to Renée?"

"Madame Dubois? That's a marvelous idea, Dodo."

"I'll write as soon as we get home."

***

As all the Dorchesters enjoyed a sublime chocolate soufflé that evening, Dodo decided to broach the subject of the car. They had just finished a marvelous dinner of roast lamb and pommes de terre au gratin in their snug, family dining room that was much less pretentious than the formal one, and there was a tangible sense of bien-être in the air, wrapping each of them like a cozy blanket. The perfect setting for entrapment.

"Didi and I got an invitation to Farrington Hall today," she said casually, examining her glossy nails and twisting a garnet ring around her slender finger.

"Did you?" burst out her mother, Lady Guinevere Dorchester. "I haven't seen Octavia in simply ages! She is *so* much fun!"

"I'm terribly excited!" gushed Didi. "It will be my first proper weekend away as a real adult!"

"Do give Tavie my love," continued Lady Guinevere, "I wonder if she's going to Ascot this year? I shall have to write."

"You could always call her on the telephone," Didi pointed out.

"That contraption is so inelegant a way to communicate," complained her mother.

"You'll take the train I suppose?" remarked Sir Alfred Dorchester, as he scraped the tiny soufflé bowl with great dedication.

"I was hoping we might take the Bentley," suggested Dodo, holding up her crystal glass with one hand as if to examine its contents as she crossed her fingers under the table with the other.

"What a splendid idea, Alfred!" said Lady Guinevere, winking at her eldest daughter.

Lord Dorchester's bushy eyebrows sank, a severe line separating them like opposing armies, his mouth puckering in disdain as though the delicious soufflé had suddenly soured. "The Bentley?" he blustered. "I don't think so, Dodo. It's quite a long journey and you don't have much experience yet."

"Nonsense!" contradicted Lady Guinevere. "Dodo just drove me all the way to Purley and she did a marvelous job, didn't you darling?"

"I did navigate very well, Daddy," she agreed, "and we didn't get lost once! Oh, won't you please let us use it?"—she paused and dropped her voice—"if I were a boy you wouldn't have any objections."

"Oh, now that is unfair!" growled her father as he wiped his bristly moustache with a rather chocolatey serviette. "I am merely concerned for your welfare."

"I know you are," she purred back, attempting to smooth his ruffled feathers, "but I've had plenty of experience now, and I'm confident that it's a journey I can easily make."

Her father continued to mutter under his breath until his wife declared, "What is the car for if not to make traveling easier, Alfred?"

All three women fixed him with dovelike stares until he crumbled. "Oh well, I suppose if you put it like that!"

Didi squeezed her eyes shut in triumph and Lady Guinevere nodded at Dodo victoriously.

"I'm going to my club!" grunted Lord Dorchester, pushing his chair back and retiring from the room in defeat.

When the door had closed, Didi let out a squeal.

"Dodo, you really should not goad him like that," her mother gently reproved, "it does nothing to help your case."

"I know, Mummy, but I get so impatient. He can be remarkably primitive in his notions."

"He'll come around," she responded. "Just give him some time. These modern ideas are evolving so quickly it's making his head spin. He still can't understand why any woman would want to wear trousers!"

"Dear Daddy," said Didi, "the world is changing too fast for him."

"A couple of hours at the club with his cronies, setting the world to rights, will do the trick!" their mother commented. "Who else will be at Farrington Hall?"

"We have no idea yet," replied Didi.

"Well, I'm sure Octavia has hand-picked the guests," said Lady Guinevere, "she is a marvel that way. Oh, to be young and swept off my feet again!"

"Did Daddy really sweep you off your feet?" asked Didi.

"I wasn't thinking of your father," Guinevere said through her laughter. "He sort of, mopped me up after a bad breakup. No, I was thinking of some of my other conquests."

Dodo looked side-long at her mother. Guinevere was a handsome woman who still turned heads, even though she had just turned forty-five. Dodo could well imagine that she had been a heartbreaker in her heyday. She was fully aware that her father had been a comfortable choice after a serious, passionate relationship had ended painfully, almost inducing an emotional breakdown. She was also mindful of the fact that her father worshiped their mother, unable to believe his luck that she had ever agreed to marry him.

The thought of young men falling at her mother's feet brought a smile to her face, especially since she had recently had her own heart broken. She had staggered away from the failed relationship, crushed and bruised.

"Oh, do tell!" begged Didi, enthralled by the very idea of romance.

Dodo opened her mouth to speak but thought better of it. *She will learn soon enough that affairs of the heart can be brutal. No need to burst her youthful innocence with my current cynicism.*

Chapter 2

Freddy Farrington

The blasted golf bag would not stand upright as Freddy tried to thrust in his club. He had just finished an atrocious round of golf, was having trouble dealing with his embarrassment, and to add insult to injury, the bloomin' bag was against him!

"Steady on old chap," said Charlie Chadwick, his golf partner for the day, "what did that bag ever do to you?"

They had been good friends since they were in knee socks and Freddy Farrington felt perfectly at ease complaining. He took a deep breath. "That's ok for you to say, you just had the round of your life! Nothing went my way today, nothing! I don't know why I play this silly game anyway!" He slapped the leather bag savagely.

"Well, it's not as though your life depended on it, old chap. It's just golf. So, you lost a small wager. You win some you lose some. Let's go and get lunch. That should cheer you up."

Freddy seared Charlie's back with a withering look. *I'll bet he doesn't have a care in the world.*

The golf bag finally submitted, and the two young men rolled their gear toward the clubhouse.

"You never told me who else is coming this weekend to your little shindig," continued Charlie.

"Did I not? I suppose I was a bit preoccupied with sand traps and water hazards! Let's see, Marcus and Julian from Cambridge—you've met them once before I think, Anita Anderson – my neighbor - and Colonel Alexander and his wife, old friends of my parents. Oh, and I almost forgot—Didi and Dodo Dorchester too."

Charlie stopped in his tracks. "You mean the dazzling Dorchester sisters! Well, well, the weekend is certainly looking up. I haven't seen Dodo for ages. She is so very fashionable these days. I hear that she has single-handedly rescued more than one fashion house on both sides of the Channel." Charlie looked into the distance. "That woman is a delight to behold. Intelligent too. I thought she was engaged or something? Saw it in the society pages."

"Oh, that's over," said Freddy.

"Really?" Charlie began to mount the steps. "That's good to know."

"Yes, they are both rather yummy, though they could not look more different in spite of the fact that they're sisters. One dark and the other fair. Ebony and ivory. I do believe they'll make the weekend very interesting."

"I used to visit their estate quite a lot as a child," mused Charlie, pushing open the restaurant door.

"Me too!" remarked Freddy, following in his wake. "Do you remember what an ugly duckling Dorothea was at thirteen?"

"Yes!" agreed Charlie, "How she bloomed. I don't think I would stand a chance with her now."

"Diantha, on the other hand, was always very pretty with her blond curls and pink lips. I had quite a crush on her when I was seventeen," admitted Freddy.

"I suspected as much." Charlie laughed, already parking his golf bag, ready to climb the stairs to the restaurant. "I wouldn't mind a shot at either one of them, though I gather they still think of me as a rambunctious schoolboy. And I remember that their father can be rather a tartar!"

"You're right!" said Freddy slapping Charlie on the back. "If he caught anyone messing with either of them, well…he's a crack shot by all accounts!"

After lunch the two men parted ways. Freddy watched Charlie leave feeling more than a little jealous of his win, before finally throwing the treasonous golf bag into the boot of his new car. He felt slightly better after the slap-up luncheon but it still rankled. Pushing down the lid of the boot he regarded the sleek, green sports car fondly. It had probably been a bad idea to buy it with everything that was going on, but cars were his guilty pleasure. The deep emerald paint contrasted so well with the shiny bumper and grill, and the smooth shapes and long lines of the body were aesthetically pleasing. He rubbed a tiny spot of lime from the bonnet with a silk handkerchief. *Such a shame I didn't win the round of golf and the bet on it!*

***

It wasn't far to Farrington Hall, and the staff were in a cacophony of cleaning in preparation for the weekend arrivals. Freddy rushed past them and straightening his cravat went in search of his parents who he found relaxing in the drawing room, taking afternoon tea.

"What ho!" he cried, with an insincerity he hoped would not be noticed. He patted the dog lying lazily by the big hearth and sunk into a comfy chair.

"Hello, dear boy," exclaimed his mother. Lady Octavia Farrington had been a beauty in her day, he knew, but that day was past, and she was content to eat whenever and whatever she wanted, trading in her slim figure for pleasant satisfaction. He loved her for it. Unlike the other chaps' mothers, she was a playful parent and an entertaining hostess—people clamored for an invitation to her parties. Life was never dull when Octavia Farrington was around.

"What have you been doing today?" she asked.

"I was playing golf with Charlie—if you can call it that. I could not make a shot for life nor limb. I really wonder why I bother with it," he said kicking the hearth in frustration.

"Ah, but it is the sport of diplomacy and business, dear one. You would do well to improve your game if you are to move forward in the world of business…or politics." She looked at him through wild, graying curls.

"Can you really see me as a politician, Mother?" he asked grinning, and just like that his toxic mood was lightened. Such was the magic of his mother's wit.

"I've never been able to master the silly game either," growled Richard Farrington, as he chewed on his pipe. "Rather go huntin' or fishin' any day."

"Amen to that, Pops! Perhaps we can encourage more politicians and businessmen to fish."

Richard Farrington stroked the voluminous, white moustache that accented his ruddy cheeks. "I'm jolly glad the Colonel and his new Missus are coming for the weekend, Tavie. I'm too old for the dancing and late nights of the young now."

"New? They've been married seven years now, my darling."

"Really? Seems new to me. Anyway, I'm jolly glad they're coming. Are they bringing that new jewel from India for us to see? Famous or something, isn't it?"

"Oh yes! It belonged to some Indian princess or some such thing," replied Lady Farrington. "Lovely! As you know, I have a bit of a thing for anything shiny. Do you suppose Anne will let me wear it?"

"Don't see why not old bean. We've known them since the year dot after all. Well, the first wife, anyway." Ensconced in an easy chair, Freddy was feeling marginally better about life now. He grabbed some tea and a biscuit and tried to shrug off the lingering irritation at losing the golf game. As his parents talked, he began thinking about the weekend ahead, considering the prospect with anticipation. The arrival of the Dorchesters was particularly appealing. A welcome distraction from his current financial concerns.

***

Charlie Chadwick

After leaving Freddy, Charlie jumped into his old, wreck of a Ford and adjusted the mirror. His eyes were not bright enough and his nose was off-center—Dodo Dorchester would never see him as a serious contender. Too bad!

He backed out of the golf club pointing his car in the direction of home, which was currently a seedy bedsit in Balham. As a third-year, student funds were low, and he hated to ask his parents for any more money. So, he made do.

His father had told him that he was always welcome at home, but he loved his independence and the privacy it afforded. When things were really tight—which was happening more and more—he would show up at home for a good meal, but he never stayed over anymore.

As he wound his way through the country lanes, he reflected on the game he had just played. Something was definitely off with Freddy, but he could not put his finger on what. Perhaps it was a woman? Freddy usually beat him easily but not today. At least Freddy's off-day meant he had won the wager—a fact his wallet was very happy about. He could fill up the car and go out for dinner.

***

Anita Anderson

Anita Anderson checked both directions before sliding along the side of the greenhouse. As she rounded the corner, she caught her white polka dot skirt on a jagged piece of glass. "Dash it all!" she cried, then slapped her hand to her mouth and waited to see if anyone had heard. Confident that she was alone, she sloped off to the folly, jogging from bush to bush for camouflage.

She crept up the steps of the Grecian structure, built fifty years before by her grandfather, and looking behind her, gently pushed open the heavy wooden door. As her eyes adjusted, she reached out her hand and it was grabbed from the dark. She was not alarmed as this was a rendezvous. The hand pulled her into an embrace as urgent lips found her own, no words being necessary.

After several delicious minutes, she pulled away. "Billy, are you sure you weren't followed?"

"I was right careful, m'lady," he said huskily, making her laugh at his pet title for her. He pulled her to the dingy sofa, a single shaft of light highlighting the dust motes swirling in the air. As he brushed her auburn hair away from her forehead, she shivered with longing. He was the first man she had ever loved, and the craving for him was like a drug addiction.

He entwined his fingers with hers and lifted their knuckles to his lips while holding her gaze. His eyes, blue as Grecian pools, drew her in until she was happily drowning. "I wish we could tell the world about us," he whispered into her hair.

"Me too," she murmured. "But you know we can't."

"I do," he sighed.

"It makes it more exciting that we have to meet in secret, don't you think?"

"Do you know how often I have wanted to tell the other lads about us? I have to bite my tongue to stop myself. Who would ever think a fellow like me could catch a proper lady like you?"

She sat back and traced a painted nail along his lower lip. "You are more worthy of my love than any other man I have ever met. It is society that puts an artificial wedge between us. Why shouldn't the classes mix when they are in love?" She dragged her finger along his firm forearm.

Billy looked at his watch. "I only have five minutes before I have to be getting back, or my boss will have my guts for garters—"

She stopped his protestations by kissing him again.

***

Marcus Makepeace

Marcus Makepeace looked around his father's club. He had come, cap in hand, to admit to some indiscretions at college. He had just told his father a rather edited version of events and was waiting for the reaction. He looked around again. The place was full of ancient specimens who looked as though they already had one foot in the grave. Good grief! He was never going to join. He wanted something with a bit more life—like those new dance clubs he'd heard about.

"Failed? What do you mean failed? A Makepeace hasn't failed his exams at Cambridge in over a century." Mortimer Makepeace glared at his offspring over the top of his *Times*.

"It wasn't my bally fault, Father," groaned Marcus. "My tutor got sick and wasn't able to bring me up to speed. I'll do the retakes in a few weeks and it will all be as it should be. Nothing to worry about."

"Well, you'd better pass them next time. We have a reputation to uphold. I got a first in the Classics, don't you know."

Don't I ever? "Well, Father," he said out loud, standing to leave, "it's been jolly to see you. Don't suppose you could give me a little cash? I've got a long weekend at old Farrington's this weekend."

His father glared at him through white, bushy eyebrows, reminding Marcus of a walrus. "What happened to your allowance?" his father growled.

"You have no idea how expensive everything is these days, Father. I mean really, it costs an arm and a leg just to have tea at *Claridge's* anymore."

His father huffed and puffed into his moustache as he extracted several notes from his wallet. Marcus grabbed them with a quick handshake and bolted.

He gulped in the London air outside the stuffy men's club and raised his face to the sunshine. That hadn't gone too badly. At least he was still alive. Good decision to edit the truth though. He scanned the street and hailed a cab.

"Kensington, please."

Several hours later, after giving the store clerk his address in Mayfair, he bounded down the steps of *Harrod's* bumping into someone who was leaping up.

"Charlotte Pennington, as I live and breathe! Well, hasn't it been an age?" The confused young woman looked up holding onto her hat. "Markie! Fancy seeing you here! Where have you been hiding? Haven't seen you at any parties recently."

"Keeping a low profile, old thing. Been swatting. Had my exams, don't you know? They were absolutely ghastly too. Failed the lot! Pater's not too happy with me right now. But the retakes aren't for a while, so I've popped down to Town to play."

"Oh, how serendipitous! I'm just rushing in here to get some stockings but then you simply must come back to the house with me. Mummy will be delighted to see you. You can come, can't you?"

"Absolutely! Lead on!" he cried.

In the early hours, Marcus emerged from the Pennington's house on Belgrave Square, much lighter in the wallet than when he had entered. He had convinced himself that it would have been rude not to join in the evening of gambling since Mrs. Pennington had specifically invited him. His head ached from a night of excess, and he found his pockets empty of any change to catch a cab.

As the sun poked its head over the horizon, his pecuniary situation compelled him to walk. He had intended to use today for revising for the upcoming exam re-sits. Of course, now he would need to sleep in preparation for his weekend at Farrington Hall.

As he crept up the back stairs to his childhood room, he passed the maids who had already risen to start work on preparing the grand house for the day. He put his finger to his lips as he slipped by, causing the younger ones to giggle.

Fatigue hit him like a wall as he walked into his darkened room, the bed beckoning to his weary body. He flopped onto it without even taking off his clothes and was soon slumbering like a baby.

The sun was high in the sky by the time he opened his eyes again. Dressing slowly, he descended the stairs in a stupor.

"We are honored that you have decided to join us, Marcus," drawled his mother, her tongue firmly planted in her cheek. Her eyes narrowed. "You look positively awful!"

Dragging his hands down his stubbled face he shook his head. "Harsh, Mother, so harsh. Is that any way to talk to your favorite son?"

"You are my *only* son, Marcus," she clarified, "and it is merely the truth. And what is this I hear about you failing your exams? Really, you are wasting your education and bringing shame on your family. What do you have to say for yourself?"

In his current condition, this interrogation was too much. "Mother, can this at least wait until after I have had some lunch, I'm starving you know, and I simply cannot think on an empty stomach." Mrs. Makepeace rolled her eyes and gritted her teeth. Marcus took this as permission to delay.

After he had consumed several bites, his mother pursued her line of questioning. "Well? How could you fail your exams?"

Marcus took a deep breath and began his rehearsed patter. "My tutor fell sick and couldn't help me study the correct things –"

"Stop right there!" she exclaimed. "That kind of clap trap may work on your father, but I was not born yesterday, Marcus. You are squandering your time playing when you should be studying. It will not do, Marcus, it will not do! You need to knuckle down and pass your retakes or there will be consequences." She said this last wagging her finger and pushing her chair back to leave the table. As she exited the room she called back over her shoulder, "Consequences, Marcus!"

Marcus returned to his room and fell back onto the bed in despair. The final drawer in the dresser in his room had not delivered any cash. How would he get to Farrington Hall? His father would not welcome another request for money.

As he lay pouting, he remembered someone mentioning Dodo and Didi Dorchester. Perhaps it was time to call them on the telephone and cadge a ride? He rang the bell and asked the butler to call the Dorchesters. From the look on his sour face, Marcus deduced that the butler was less than amused by the commission. "Indeed, sir."

After fifteen minutes had passed, the butler returned. "Lady Dorothea Dorchester is on the telephone, sir." He withdrew like a specter. Marcus galloped down the stairs to the telephone room.

"Dodo? That you old thing?"

"Marcus. How *are* you?" Was she less than happy to hear from him or was he imagining things?

"I'm fine thanks. Look, I'll get right to it. I heard that you were invited to Farrington Hall for the weekend, and I was wondering if we might go down together?"

"Oh!" There was a pause. "Did you want to come and get us?"

"Ah, well that's the thing. I'm without wheels at the moment and was wondering if you would have room for one more?"

"Trusting a female to drive you? How *brave* of you, Marcus. Alright then, we'll pick you up Thursday evening at five, sharp. You'll be ready, won't you? I don't like to drive in the dark."

"Perfect. You are marvelous, Dodo. See you Thursday."

Chapter 3

Julian Jeffries

Julian Jeffries emerged from the dance hall, a pretty young thing hanging on his arm, as the sun was just beginning its daily climb. He propped her against the railing and dragged his hands down his face, shaking his head to clear it. It had been a long but very pleasant evening. Just the distraction he had needed.

He ran to the curb and hailed a passing taxi and then bundled himself and the stylish young woman into the back as she giggled and tucked her hand into the crook of his arm.

"Little Barton," he told the driver and then slumped back, finally succumbing to fatigue.

"Address?" barked the taxi driver after what seemed like mere seconds. Julian squinted, trying to remember the address. Catching a glimpse of the young woman who was softly snoring, her lipstick smudged on her delicate chin, he grinned. "Thurston Lodge," he managed.

The taxi swung to the left causing his stomach to lurch, and he closed his eyes waiting for the unexpected wave of nausea to pass. The feeling had revived uncomfortable memories.

Within minutes, the cab pulled up onto the gravel of his family home and Julian stumbled out, searching in his jacket for some money to pay his fare. He pulled out his pocket lining, finding nothing.

Leaning into the back of the taxi he barked, "Serena?" When she did not respond he shook her shoulder. "Serena," he repeated. "Do you have any cash?"

The deep frown of confusion shadowed her good looks, and she wiped her mouth in a most unfeminine gesture further smearing the red lipstick. "Cash?" she queried as though he were speaking in a foreign tongue.

"Yes, you know, money, to pay the cabbie." And he tilted his head toward the front of the car. She peered around the leather interior of the vehicle looking confused, as though she had woken up in a dream.

"Oh, never mind!" he said with contempt and staggered to the front door. He had hoped to slink in with little disturbance, but the wretched door was locked, and he was forced to ring the bell.

After what seemed like an eternity, a disheveled butler opened the door in his pajamas. "Young Mr. Jeffries!" he said in shock. "What are you doing here at this hour?" The old servant squinted and peered behind Julian in disgust.

"I need some cash for the cab. Do be a good man and give me some." Humphries, the butler, closed one eye and breathed in deeply searching for an ounce of patience then left and returned with the necessary funds. "Oh, jolly good!" said Julian and hopped back down the stairs.

Serena had slumped over and was sound asleep again. To the cabbie he said, "Please take her to Lower Piddleton." He gave an address then slammed the door closed and the taxi scrunched away over the gravel.

When Julian turned back, the butler had disappeared, but the door was ajar, so he crept in and climbed up to the room his mother kept for him. As he drifted off, he thought that he would get a well-deserved tongue lashing from his mother the next day, but he was too tired to care.

***

"Really Jules, at your age you should be more responsible! Poor Humphries is exhausted. Whatever were you thinking?" Julian had woken late, horribly hung over and was now being interrogated by his mother in the drawing room. He was reconsidering his decision to come to his parent's place instead of going home. He kicked the edge of the deep Persian rug.

"I wasn't," he grumbled. "Thinking, that is."

"Clearly," his mother responded tartly. "But now that you are here, what have you been doing with yourself lately?"

Julian Jeffries knew this was code for 'have you met a nice girl yet?' and grimaced. Then his mind, that was still awakening, caught onto a memory that he knew his mother would approve of.

"Not much, but I have been invited to Farrington Hall this weekend and the much- heralded Dorchester sisters will be there, or so I'm told." He let the arrow fly, watching it hang, causing his mother's expression to undergo a remarkable recovery.

"Lady Dorothea and Lady Diantha? Oh, now *there* are some lovely girls and from such a good family. Have you ever met them?"

"Not that I remember." He flicked some lint from his trousers and stroked his moustache.

"If you play your cards right, Jules, you could marry one of them!" She looked over at him with an appraising eye. "Well, you would need to have a haircut and shave and dress a little more carefully, but I think you would clean up well enough."

He clutched his heart. "Mother, you cut me. Such criticism from the woman who gave birth to me. Am I that much of a mess? Wait—don't answer that. I'm going out to get my hair cut."

***

Octavia and Richard Farrington

Octavia Farrington's hand draped over the side of the wicker chair in which she was reclining on the south patio. She was snoring.

"Octavia," said her husband with concern, as he pushed through the French doors to the patio, noticing the letter lying on the floor by her chair. He scooped it up and put it in his pocket. "Tavie, it is not yet ten in the morning, and you are already tipsy!"

His wife raised her head as though it weighed a ton and peered through bleary eyes at her husband. "Whaat?" she gurgled, dragged from a peaceful, albeit drunken, slumber.

"Tavie, I really think you might have a problem, my dear."

"Nonsense, Richard," replied Octavia, as though she had several grapes in her mouth. "I am not drunk, just a bit woozy, that's all."

He sat down beside his wife and fondly took her hand. "I'm worried about you."

"I have it all perfectly under control, old thing. It was just such a lovely morning, and I felt like a tipple out here in the sun. Then I had a couple more and the next thing I know you are dragging me awake from a very pleasant nap." He noticed that she did not mention the letter.

Richard Farrington stroked his wife's hand affectionately and changed the subject. "I was coming to see how many RSVP's we've had so that I can have plenty of equipment for activities for the weekend."

"Everyone, darling," Octavia slurred, "everyone can come. Won't it be…fun…" she sighed as she fell back to sleep.

Richard Farrington had served as a Brigadier General in the Great War and continued in civilian life very much as he had during the war. Efficiency, preparedness and order were his bywords. The staff in the house were run like his troops.

He rose, looking down at his wife affectionately. They say that opposites attract and that had been true for him. He had met Octavia at the turn of the century. She had been just nineteen when she had splashed onto the social scene with her beauty and free-spirited nature. He had been completely captivated.

Theirs had been a happy marriage, full of love and social whirl. She had been nothing but an asset. Until now. Until the awful letters.

Recently, she had embarrassed herself in public on more than one occasion with her drinking, and he cringed for what it was doing to her reputation. Their reputation. Their boy had flown the nest and with his own army career behind him, Richard had felt the call to public service. He was seriously considering running for parliament. Having a lush for a wife would not help those ambitions.

To distract himself, he went to his library to go over the agenda for the long weekend. Octavia had come up with the program. Thursday evening was to be cocktails on the terrace after dinner and then an evening of dancing—Octavia had said it was the best way to start the weekend off with a bang. Friday there was a plan to play golf during the day with charades in the evening, followed by a grand game of croquet on Saturday, a large dinner, cards and billiards. Sunday would be a slow day with a lazy lunch before people left to go home.

The motivation for this weekend had been their son, Freddy. He had no desire to follow his father into the military and had not done well in school. Richard had needed to pull some strings to get him a job and help him move into a flat in town, but he had heard through the grapevine that things were not going well. This had caused them a great deal of anxiety. Octavia thought a party weekend might cheer Freddy up.

With his thoughts pre-occupied he turned to the stack of mail on his desk and finding his letter opener, slit open the top envelope.

I know what you did. The now familiar lettering screamed from the page just like all the others. His insides churned. The letters had been cut from various publications as usual and were clumsily pasted to a single sheet of paper. He dropped the offensive article as though it had been a cobra.

***

Arthur and Anne Alexander

"A bit further to the right," shouted Mrs. Alexander as she attempted to take the Colonel's picture. She had received the new camera for her birthday and was learning how to use it.

The Colonel was standing by his favorite horse next to the beech tree and she was trying to get a shot she could give him to put on his desk.

"That's it!" she cried, "Lovely, darling! One, two, three smile!"

She dropped the camera back around her neck and came toward him as he walked his horse across the grounds to the stable. She pulled her cardigan around her as a stiff breeze kicked up.

"That was marvelous, dearest," she said, giving her husband a peck on the cheek. "Torbin is so photogenic. I bet you look pretty good too!" she continued, putting her arm through the Colonel's as they left the stable.

"Are we all ready to go to the Farrington's this weekend?" he asked.

"Pretty much. Just a few odds and ends to add."

The Colonel was fifteen years older than his second wife, Anne. His first wife had died before the Great War and the battle action in France had filled his days and mind. However, when the war ended there was no ignoring the emptiness of the house, and he had plunged into a state of depression. Octavia Farrington, concerned, had arranged one of her magical dinner parties and invited a lovely young woman named Anne and seated her beside him. The rest was history.

Anne was very fond of jewelry; unique pieces that increased in value and made tremendous investments. Together they had started a collection of exotic items, traveling the world in search of one-of-a-kind creations. Having both inherited from wealthy parents, they had initially been quite able to travel wherever the search for jewels took them. Though things had changed it was a hard habit to break.

"I'm going to take the new emerald necklace we got in Indonesia. Tavie is dying to see it," she added.

"Ah! The star of our collection," he said thoughtfully. "I thought that chap in Indonesia was never going to sell it to us! He looked like he might take the money and cut our throats!"

"He was rather frightening, I do remember," she agreed. "I was very glad it was midday and not in a dark alley somewhere."

"I believe it was your feminine wiles that saved the day"—He ran his finger along her cheek—"and he could not deny that you were the perfect model. The jewel sat upon your neck as though it had been commissioned. I even think he was a little in love with you by the end of the transaction."

"You do exaggerate, darling. I am far too fair for his tastes I would wager." Anne reached out for his hand. "Do you remember the tale he told us of its provenance? Now that we have had it for some months, do you put any stock in the supposed curse upon it?"

"No! Stuff and nonsense. Curse indeed!" blustered the Colonel. "But its heritage does make for an interesting dinner story. An Indonesian princess whose lover murdered her for the jewel, and a mother who cursed the lover and the jewels when it was discovered. Fascinating!"

Anne was having more trouble dismissing the tale, the curse nagged at her, though she loved the necklace. She turned to face her husband, looking him straight in the eyes. "Do you really think it possible that someone could love jewels more than people, darling? It seems rather far-fetched."

Arthur placed his hand on her shoulder. "People have murdered for far less, my dear. You have to remember that you live in a very civilized time, the Great War notwithstanding, but it has not always been so."

"I suppose you are right." She shivered, wrapping the cardigan more tightly around her. "Let's go inside for some tea."

Chapter 4

Dodo honked the horn repeatedly as her car swept into the gravel driveway of Pennington Place, and a butler in a severely pressed suit appeared wearing a look that positively dripped with disapproval. He stepped ponderously down the stone steps, his bald head down and crunched over to the Bentley. Dodo wound down the window and leaned out.

"We have come to collect Mr. Marcus," she explained. "Lady Dorothea and Lady Diantha Dorchester." The butler underwent a complete and instantaneous metamorphosis upon realizing *who* had summoned him in such a modern fashion.

"Of course!" he said, in the perfect diction that only butlers can achieve. "Please be assured that had I known Lord and Lady Dorchester's daughters were anticipated, I would have been ready and waiting." He managed to sound both subservient and condescending.

"Well, we aren't staying, so I don't believe we were expected," said Dodo, flipping her glossy hair. "We are simply here to pick up Markie." The butler winced at the contraction of the name.

"I shall inform Mr. Marcus that you are here," said the butler as he bowed away from the car with deference towards the tasteful mansion house.

"How on earth did we get roped into taking Marcus?" moaned Didi. "He is a perfect brat! What was Octavia thinking in inviting him?"

"He called and asked for a ride," replied Dodo staring out at the manicured hedges. "I wanted to make an excuse, but I couldn't come up with a plausible one on the spot. He is a bally bore. Octavia must be slipping in her old age," she mused. "Marcus used to be fun, but in the last few years he has become so self-centered."

"Perhaps Freddy insisted," said Didi. "They have always been pretty close, haven't they?"

Five long minutes passed as Dodo tapped the steering wheel, looking up at the threatening clouds. Finally, the butler reappeared with a footman carrying several bags. The footman placed the bags on the luggage rack.

"Mr. Marcus will be right down," simpered the butler, his brow wrinkling, reminding Dodo of a Shar-pei dog. "Is there anything else I can do for you?"

"If you would be a dear and tell him to get a move on," Dodo said, flashing her straight, white teeth in a dazzling smile. It had its usual affect and the butler softened, bowed and retreated.

Five more agonizing minutes passed as the clouds turned gray and heavy.

"Where *is* that man!" Dodo groaned, honking the horn again. "I thought it was women that were supposed to keep everybody waiting!"

"Shall I just go and get him?" asked Didi.

"Yes, why don't you. I want to get on the road before the storm comes. I detest driving in the rain especially when it gets dark."

Didi opened the car door just as the magnificent door to Pennington Place opened and Marcus exited looking as though he had all the time in the world.

"What on *earth* took you so long!" said Dodo in exasperation.

"Oh, have you been waiting long?" replied Marcus, completely ignorant to that fact that he had inconvenienced the sisters. Dodo skewered him up with a look that could freeze fire, but he was all innocence and oblivion. She sighed. "Well, you are here now. Haven't forgotten anything, have you?" This last was said with tongue in cheek as the four bags residing on the luggage rack dwarfed hers and Didi's. *They* had each brought one bag and one hat box.

"No, no I think I have everything," he said, completely insensible that she had jibed him. Dodo flung a caustic look back at her sister who had moved to the back seat at Marcus's insistence.

The first hour took them out of the city and before much further they were sailing along country roads. Dodo felt the annoyance that had settled in her shoulders melt away. And then Marcus opened his mouth and began regaling them with off-key songs from Cambridge and the stiffness returned. His renditions sorely tested the sisters' powers of patience and good manners. Dodo gripped the steering wheel ever tighter and gritted her teeth.

A few more miles sped by when the sky suddenly darkened with black rainclouds and they heard a distressing pop as the right side of the car lurched. Large raindrops began to slap the windshield. Dodo pressed the brake and swerved onto the side of the road. She jumped out to see what had happened as an inquisitive cow idled over. "Oh blast!" she yelled, "It's a flat!"

"Do you know what to do?" asked Didi of Marcus, who was still sitting, ungallantly in his seat.

"Not a chance," said Marcus. "I'm hopeless at that kind of thing." Didi caught her sister's glance and rolled her eyes in the direction of Marcus, while opening her door.

"Have you done this before, Dodo?" she asked.

"Once. Let's see if I can remember." She strode to the back of the car and opened the boot looking for some kind of tool that might jar her memory. A swift crack of thunder caused her to jump and hit her head on the boot lid. "Dash it all!" she exclaimed as she rubbed her crown. "Didi, there's an umbrella on the floor in the back. Be a dear and get it for me."

The umbrella was retrieved and Didi held it over her sister's head as she searched for the jack. "Voila!" said Dodo with a flourish, brandishing the elusive item. Marcus remained firmly ensconced in the comfort of the Bentley.

Both sisters huddled under the umbrella, sizing up the offensive tire, hopelessly trying to figure out how to position the jack, when another car honked its horn and came to a stop. The rain was now coming down in sheets and it was hard to see the driver. In moments, he had jumped out of his car with the collar of his jacket up and a hat plonked on his head to keep out the rain.

"Charlie!" exclaimed Dodo, on catching a glimpse of his face. "Oh, what a knight in shining armor you are! I can't remember how to use the silly thing, and this rain is making everything awful."

"Stand back and I'll take care of it," he said. The two girls gladly did as they were told. Didi knocked on the passenger side window and Marcus reluctantly wound the window down a couple of inches.

"You'll have to get out," she said.

"But it's raining."

"Charlie Chadwick is here, and he's going to change the tire. You'll have to get out."

Marcus wound the window back up and slowly opened the door, ducking his head as if that would stop the rain falling on it. He nodded at Charlie who was already on the ground, pumping up the jack.

"Don't you have a mackintosh in one of your bags?" Dodo asked Marcus.

"Ah, no," he said, "wasn't expecting rain."

"This is England, Markie," Dodo scolded, "one should always expect rain."

Marcus pushed his way under the umbrella, causing both girls to edge out and suffer the drips from the umbrella falling on their shoulders. They exchanged exasperated looks behind his back.

Another crack of thunder followed by a large flash of lightning had Marcus jumping out of his skin. Before she could prevent herself, Dodo snorted and it was all she could do to stop laughing out loud. Didi's lip curled.

As they waited, Dodo looked down at her new, white, leather shoes, now splattered with mud. She hoped the maids at Farrington Hall were up to the task of returning them to their pristine condition.

"All done!" said Charlie, jumping up and sending a spray of rain off his coat and onto the trio under the umbrella.

"About time! I'm soaked!" grumbled Marcus and shot back into the car.

"Thank you!" shouted Dodo over the noise of the pelting rain. "We owe you one!" Charlie nodded and turned back to his car. "I'll see you at the Hall," he said as he slid into the cracked leather seat, closed his door, and roared off.

The two sisters retreated to the Bentley. Within seconds the aroma of wet wool and moth balls filled the air, causing Didi to wrinkle her nose. Dodo started the car again, and they pulled out onto the road in the furious storm.

"What luck that Charlie happened by!" said Dodo as the wipers fought valiantly to clear the windshield of moisture.

"I suppose so," managed Marcus, "but he could have moved more quickly. My slacks are sodden."

"Well, *I* think he's marvelous, rescuing us like that," purred Didi.

Marcus' ears turned pink. Dodo hoped his conscience was pricking him.

***

"Welcome to Farrington Hall," said the Farrington's butler in all his formal splendor as he held open the great front door. Dodo felt her wet clothing sticking to her legs and hoped she wasn't dripping on the black and white tiles. "I will show the gentlemen up to their rooms and Mrs. McCreedy will show the ladies to theirs. Did either of you gentlemen bring a valet?" This last was directed at Marcus and Charlie, who had arrived just before them.

"Heavens, no!" cried Charlie. "Whoever brings a valet anymore?"

"You would be surprised, Mr. Chadwick," said the butler, his words drawn out in a ponderous, judgmental tone. "And ladies? Did you bring a maid?"

"Yes, but she's arriving on the five o'clock train. Will that be a problem?" Lizzie was someone they could not live without.

"Not at all. I shall send a driver to fetch her and make a room ready in the eaves. This way gentlemen." He led the way up the enormous, sweeping stairs.

Mrs. McCreedy was just about to take the sisters up when Octavia burst into the entry and almost bowled them over with a great hug. "But my darlings, we expected you ages ago! I was quite worried when the storm started. I took a bath to take my mind off worrying and now here you are!"

"We got a flat tire," explained Dodo, returning the hug, "and if Charlie hadn't helped us out, we would have been even later!"

"My goodness! You are soaked through. I do wish they would invent a better tire. Far too many go flat in my opinion. Still prefer the train, myself. Now, go on up and get settled and then join us for drinks. Julian and Anita are already here—you remember Anita, Dodo? As are the Alexanders. They all arrived just after lunch. See you in a pip!" And she floated away on a whiff of brandy.

So Julian Jeffries was here. Interesting.

The sisters were shown to connecting rooms that each had its own bathroom—a very luxurious thing, even for the gentry. Most old mansions had a bathroom on each floor or wing that guests were obliged to share.

As Dodo stripped off her wet clothing, she looked out onto the dripping scenery. Thankfully, the rain had stopped but had left everything appearing heavy. Her window faced the manicured lawn with a pond, and a stone patio that seemed rather sad in the current wet conditions. Farther out, she could see the wooded area she had explored as a child. Happy memories tumbled over each other.

Her room was rather old fashioned for her more modern tastes, but it was comfortable with an eiderdown that looked very inviting. She was feeling tired and strained across her shoulders from the drive in the steady rain and encroaching darkness. A bath would have to wait she supposed, but it did call to her like a siren. A long hot, soak was just the ticket. She sighed.

Later.

"My room is just like yours," said Didi, opening the connecting door and peering in, "only where yours is rose, mine is violet. Mother would simply love it!"

"I was just eyeing the bath," admitted Dodo, picking through her bag for a cozy wrap to wear. "I feel in need of warming up and something to help me shed my irritation with Marcus. He is such a wet blanket! I think his character is deteriorating with age—he was never this bad as a child."

"I expect he was smothered," said Didi sagely. "You know, a mother who did everything for him—or got the servants to. He really is rather useless. And so self-absorbed. He wasn't even grateful that Charlie helped us!"

"I know! I was shocked. It rather got under my skin."

"Well, you did a good job of not showing it. I do hope he is not going to be like that all weekend."

"Agreed. Anyway, Freddy will knock him out of it and Julian will be here for diversion. I don't think you have ever met him. He's rather delicious. At least he was. I haven't seen him in forever. I had rather a crush on him last time we met. I must have only been seventeen at the time. He was nineteen. I don't think he even noticed me. You were still at school."

"Well, even if he was blind to your charms before he will certainly notice you now, Dodo. Do you think we should change for dinner?"

Dodo looked down at her wrap and the pile of soiled shoes, stained white slacks and damp blouse. "Oh, dash it yes! I'm a wreck. I need to get into something clean and fresh but I just want to relax in my robe and sit in a chair for a minute. Then we can help each other change since Lizzie won't be here till later. Is that alright?"

"Of course." Didi slipped back to her room and reappeared fifteen minutes later wearing a sleek polka dot dress that slid off one shoulder.

"Julian might not notice me if you're wearing *that*!" said Dodo with a laugh. "You'll knock everyone's socks off."

"Well, I want to make a good impression." Didi grinned. "I have to shed that 'little sister' image."

Dodo, now somewhat refreshed, stood and opened her case. After looking through the clothes she held up a deep crimson dress that fell straight from the shoulders in the latest style and sported tassels that hung to the calf. She grabbed a matching headdress with a feather held in place by a crystal.

"Oh, you'll make a splash in that!" said Didi. "Julian, beware!"

Chapter 5

As the sisters came down the stairs for drinks, they heard voices in the vestibule.

"Yes, absolutely ghastly weather!" said a woman. "I know I'm close, but I am so grateful you sent the car to get me. My shoes would have been caked in mud! And my hair! Heavens!"

When the girls landed at the bottom, Octavia rushed over to make the introductions. "Ladies, do you remember Anita? Her father's estate is the next one over. I suppose it's been years…"

Dodo put out her hand. "Of course, I remember Anita. I believe we got caught stealing sugar from the kitchen many years ago."

"My goodness! I haven't thought of that in a long time." She returned Dodo's handshake with a limp grip. She had blossomed into a pretty girl in the intervening years, but her lipstick clashed terribly with her red hair and Dodo resisted the urge to grimace.

"This is my little sister, Didi—though I ought to stop calling her that as she is not very little anymore! She would have been very young back then." Anita and Didi loosely shook hands with no signs of recognition.

"Well, darlings, you all look delicious. What fabulous figures you have. Mine disappeared so long ago I've quite forgotten it! Come on, let's find something to drink. Julian is already in the drawing room." Octavia winked and Dodo and Didi exchanged a look. Dodo's stomach performed a pleasant flip.

As they entered the room, her eye went directly to Julian who was standing next to Marcus. He sported a mustache, which did nothing to detract from his handsome face, and wore his thick, sandy hair combed back. He was dressed for leisure in cream trousers and a cricket sweater. *Mmm…better than I remembered.* His eyes widened ever so slightly as she approached.

"I seem to be a little over-dressed," she said, while allowing him to take her hand and place a soft kiss upon it.

"Octavia told me not to bother dressing for dinner, but I'm very glad *you* did," he added. He held her hand just long enough to signal that the attraction was mutual.

"May I introduce my sister, Miss Diantha Dorchester."

Julian dragged his eyes away from hers and politely took Didi's hand. "She was at school when we met, years ago," added Dodo.

He turned to her with a question on his brow. "We've met before? I'm sure I would remember." Her mood took a southerly turn. "Yes, I was a gangly seventeen-year-old, and we were at Ascot or somewhere. I am not surprised you don't remember," she said, though in truth he had taken a swing at her pride.

"I've seen you in the papers, of course," he said, clearly trying to repair any offense, but the damage was done.

Octavia moved into the scene. "And you remember Anita from next door?"

"Yes, of course," replied Julian, which made the sting even worse.

"Marcus, you know everyone I think," continued Octavia. Marcus nodded but stayed where he was, cradling his drink. *Dreadful manners.*

"Now, what will you all have?"

The next five minutes were taken up with Octavia making cocktails during which the door opened, and Freddy and Charlie entered. There were kisses all around.

Just before the dinner gong, the door opened again, and the butler announced Colonel and Mrs. Alexander.

The woman's appearance was swallowed up by the enormous emerald necklace she was wearing. It positively winked in the candlelight.

Finally, Mr. Farrington arrived, apologizing for his tardy appearance.

Dodo went to stand by the fire where she could observe all the guests from afar while she nursed her bruised ego. Didi was deep in conversation with Julian, but it did not ignite any jealousy, for anyone could tell from his body language that he was not romantically interested in her sister—not that there was any reason why he shouldn't be—she looked stunning. Her gaze fell on the

Farringtons and the Alexanders. It was obvious that Mrs. Alexander was the second Mrs. Alexander, but other than the ostentatious jewelry, Dodo had to admit she was very nicely dressed. The fashion expert in her approved of the simple cream dress—it set off the jewels beautifully as it did not compete with them. The level of comfort they exhibited proved that the two couples were old friends of longstanding.

Her eyes swept over to Anita who was talking to Freddy and Charlie. Charlie was a friend to everybody and quite at ease in social situations and Freddy and Anita had known each other all their lives. From his gestures, Dodo guessed that Charlie was telling them about fixing the flat tire in the rain.

Marcus sat alone in a comfortable chair, enjoying his drink, people watching. She noted that his gaze lingered on Didi. Dodo glanced between the two. *Not a chance.*

***

"I recently got back from the West Indies," said Julian, who had been seated next to her at dinner. Dodo was still smarting from the slight, but he was being careful to be overly solicitous in an attempt to make amends and she was warming. And he smelled heavenly. As dinner progressed, they talked and he would dip his head, tipping it intimately to hers so that occasionally their hair would touch, sparking a pleasant chemistry.

She watched as he fingered his spoon with long, masculine fingers, in a slightly nervous manner suggesting that his interest in her was more than casual. She had the upper hand. It felt good. Time to throw him a line.

"How marvelous! What is it like?" Dodo rested her chin on her fist giving him her full attention.

Encouraged, he continued, "It's hard to find phrases that describe the deep blue of the sea, mere words just don't do it justice. The sand on the shores is so white that it is the perfect contrast to the blue of the water—the sun never stops shining."

"Sounds heavenly," she said, moving her blood red nails like a scarlet spider, across the tablecloth, close to his. "What took you there? Pleasure?"

"No, I have a business interest there. Well, someone has invited me to join in one."

"How fortunate! You'll get to go back. What bliss! The farthest I go these days is Paris and it can be so dreadfully cold and gloomy."

"What do you do in Paris?" He was looking at her hand adjacent to his.

"I have lots of friends there, but I visit the House of Dubois, mostly. For some reason Renée Dubois values my opinion on their new designs."

"I can see why." He smiled. "You do have a certain flair, Lady Dorothea."

Okay, I am very close to completely forgiving him.

"Oh, enough of the titles! Please, call me Dodo."

He laughed. "If you insist, *Dodo.*" He murmured her name with such heat that it made her tingle.

Better be careful, take it slowly.

She withdrew her hand from the linen tablecloth and fingered her necklace. Time to change the subject. "How do *you* know the Farringtons?" she asked.

"Freddy and I were at school together. We were in the second eleven for cricket. And you?"

"Our families have been friends since before I was born. We would visit at least once a year. I met Anita when we were children a few times, and Marcus and Charlie run in the same social circles as us."

"Lucky men," said Julian.

Fully thawed, Dodo rewarded his compliment with the full force of her most dazzling smile. He cleared his throat.

"And what does your social circle do for fun, Dodo?" he continued.

She opened her hands expressively, pressed them together and settled them against her chin as she responded "Fun? We go dancing, to the opera, the theater, play tennis and golf. How about you?"

"I enjoy all those things. I'm surprised we haven't bumped into each other before."

"But we have," she reminded him, and he had the good grace to look sheepish. "Tell me about sailing."

He grasped at the topic to cover his embarrassment. "It's like nothing else. Sea breeze on one's face, the spray of the ocean, the thrill of the adventure. I think that's why I'm drawn to the West Indies. The weather is so good for sailing—except when there is a hurricane, of course."

"Have you experienced one?"

"There was a tropical storm while I was out there, which is not as strong, but it was pretty frightening. I should hate to actually be there during a full-blown one. Did you know they can flatten hotels?"

She did know but he was being so sweet that she didn't want to admit it. "My goodness, it sounds awful and terribly exciting all at the same time!"

"Have you ever sailed?" he asked, placing his hand close to her plate in a kind of invitation. She ignored it.

"No, never. The closest I've come is punting on the Cam!"

"Then I shall have to introduce you to the sport some time." He grabbed his spoon.

"Absolutely! I shall look forward to it!"

Dodo glanced down the table in time to see Didi shoot her a strangled plea for help. She was seated next to Marcus who was droning on about something or other and Didi appeared ready to bop him on the head with her plate. Just then, Octavia saved her by rising to indicate that the ladies should withdraw.

The furniture in the drawing room had been moved back to make room for dancing later. Dodo and Didi settled into a plump sofa.

"It's just as well we came in here," Didi said heatedly. "I was about ready to excuse myself to the bathroom in desperation! What a self-centered chump Marcus is! He never let me get a word in edgeways and when I turned the other way to talk to Mr. Farrington, he kept interrupting!"

"Sorry," said Dodo. "As for me, I had a lovely time."

"I noticed," said Didi, her lip curling.

"Was it that obvious?"

"Only to me," Didi assured her.

The men entered a short while later and Freddy began fiddling with the gramophone.

When he eventually got everything working, a Charleston belted out from the machine and Julian hurried over to ask Dodo if she would care to dance. A welcome sense of contentment distilled over her. This reaction was evidence that she was truly over 'what's-his-name' and ready to embark on a new adventure. Her experience had been a painful lesson and she had worried that it would make her hard-hearted. Julian might prove to be the final stage of her cure. As they stood up, she tapped Freddy on the shoulder. "Be a darling and go and save poor Didi. Marcus has just bored her to death over dinner, and he looks ready to pounce on her for the dancing."

Freddy obligingly high-tailed it over and just managed to elbow Marcus out. Didi sent her sister a grateful smile and then turned her attention to Freddy. Charlie asked Anita to dance leaving Marcus alone to brood in a chair.

"So sorry for the odd number, Marcus," yelled Octavia over the music. "We had asked another young lady to come, but she had to cancel at the last minute." He nodded, disconsolately, and Dodo had the impression of a spoiled child being told he could not have another toy.

After the energetic Charleston, everyone flopped onto the chairs and Mr. Farrington hurried to get drinks, while Freddy found something a little slower.

"Care to dance again?" asked Julian, smiling so that his neat moustache framed his straight, white teeth. Dodo's stomach clenched with excitement and she lifted her hand so that he might pull her from the chair.

As they swung together, he pulled her close, placing his firm palm in the small of her back and gently holding her hand in his, cradling it to his chest. She allowed her head to rest on his shoulder and realized that she had missed this kind of tenderness. She surrendered to the warm feelings his closeness evoked.

When the music stopped Julian made no move to break away.

"I say," she heard Charlie complain from a distance, "let us other chaps have a chance, old boy."

After a beat, Julian released her.

"Yes, of course," he said, his voice raspy and ragged.

Freddy found another quick number and Charlie grabbed Dodo's hand, pulling her into the Black Bottom. She threw a quick apology to Julian, who was sitting out, and then flung back her head, abandoning herself to the quick steps. It was fun to dance so energetically with Charlie, but though he was very handsome, she felt no tug of attraction for him as she had for Julian.

For the rest of the evening the music remained upbeat and everyone swapped partners regularly so that no one had to sit out for too long. Dodo even danced with Marcus though he stepped on her toes more than once and talked about himself the entire time. Then, before everyone retired for the night, Freddy played another slow tune. Dodo found herself hoping that Julian would seek her out so that when he dashed across the room as if to claim a prize, she was as excited as a schoolgirl. Ready to be back in his embrace she melted into his arms eagerly. *So much for taking things slow.*

When the song ended, he twirled her around and kissed her hand, keeping his eyes on hers as he did so, his brooding gaze charged with possibilities.

"Until tomorrow, Lady Dorothea." The use of her formal name did not bother her in the least this time.

"Goodnight, Mr. Jeffries," she replied in kind, surprised to find her voice deeper than usual, her heart beating more rapidly. She cast a sultry look over her shoulder as she and Didi left the room and found him still looking.

As the door closed, Didi whispered, "Wow! I think I just got electrocuted by the electricity crackling between you two."

"He is rather attractive," Dodo admitted, "But I'm nervous that I'm jumping in with both feet like a fool. I should be more careful perhaps? You can be my voice of reason, Didi."

"Well, if you want my opinion, I think you should go for it!" Didi said.

"You think so?"

"Absolutely!" She grabbed her sister's arm. "He's gorgeous."

"What about you?" Dodo asked. "Anyone take your fancy?"

"Charlie is quite nice and such a lovely chap, but I don't know if he's interested."

"Well, the weekend has only just begun," replied Dodo.

"One thing is for sure," continued Didi, "I'm going to lose weight trying to avoid Marcus!"

Chapter 6

Row upon row of white, gauze curtains floated in front of Dodo, beckoning. As she parted one, another layer seemed to appear, hinting at a hazy figure far in the distance. A hunger to reach the elusive specter filled her. Pressing forward, her fingers brushed along the eternal, sheer veils. Dodo toiled on. And on. The ghostly shadow lingered on the far horizon always out of reach. As her knees weakened, she fought to continue her quest, pushing through fatigue and desperation. Ever moving, never progressing, the haunting presence always just a few curtains away. Just as failure threatened, Dodo saw the fleeting silhouette hurtle through the white, cold space like lightning. Strands of linen flowed from its head like a ghastly shroud, revealing the black hollows of a skull. Wrenching away from it, she screamed...

Heart thumping, head spinning, drenched in perspiration, it took a moment to realize that it had been a nightmare. The image of the skull still burned in Dodo's memory. As her blood pressure began to fall, her tense, sticky body relaxed. She lay in repose, catching her breath and turned her head to look toward the window. She had neglected to draw the curtains the night before and was therefore rewarded with a comforting view of azure blue sky studded with puffy clouds.

She rarely had nightmares, rarely dreamed actually, and the frightful experience left her feeling like a drowning kitten who had been pulled from a watery grave. Perhaps she had eaten something that did not agree with her last night.

Dodo rolled over, enjoying the plumpness of the down pillow and wrapped the silky sheets around her. To chase away the lagging memories of the dream, she thought back to the romance of the evening before. Conjuring an image of Julian's face, remembering his gentle touch, her stomach flipped again with attraction and excitement. *Was she ready for this again?* Her heart said yes. She ignored her head.

She'd had two serious relationships since her eighteenth birthday. With the first she had believed herself in love, whereas she later realized that she had merely been infatuated with the idea of romance—in love with the notion of being in love. Then her best friend Maudie had reported seeing him with another girl at a coming out ball. Her Cinderella world had crumbled.

That first heartbreak had taught her to be more guarded with her heart the second time. When Tommy Thompson had been invited to join their table at Ascot by her father, she spoke little. Tommy had recently returned from America and her father had been eager to hear of the automobile industry there. Dodo had been bored out of her mind by the talk of chassis and headlights. Tommy must have noticed and had saved her by asking if she would like to go to a play in town that evening. Without appearing over-eager she had agreed. It happened to be a play she was interested in seeing.

Tommy's intellectual curiosity had intrigued her that night. He was intelligent and funny and a perfect gentleman. When he asked her out again, she had jumped at the chance. His persistence had paid off and after several months, she had fallen hopelessly in love.

Assuming that he felt the same way, she had hinted at making their relationship more committed. She was shocked when he had laughed at her naiveté. Didn't she realize that he was going to take the world by storm? He couldn't be shackled to a wife! She berated herself for being fooled again. It had taken her a long time to recover.

In response, she had dated a string of shallow men in short order. She wondered where Julian would fall in the spectrum.

***

When she and Didi finally made it down to breakfast, they found that they were not the last. Octavia and Marcus were missing. She scanned the room for Julian and was satisfied to see his eyes light up at the sight of her. She had taken a great deal of care with her toilette, choosing a peach color chiffon blouse, paired with a cream linen skirt. She had tied the outfit together with a floral scarf around her ebony hair.

"Everyone ready for a round of golf?" asked Mr. Farrington, putting down his newspaper. "The weather is promising to be perfect."

Dodo thought she heard a quiet groan from Freddy but when she shifted her eyes to him, he was smiling along with everyone else.

As they were leaving the breakfast room, Octavia arrived, bumping into Anita who was just in front of Dodo, again trailing a strong whiff of whiskey. Dodo checked her watch; ten thirty in the morning.

The golf course was a short drive away and the weather really was splendid. Bulbous, puffy clouds highlighted the blue of the sky. Both Dodo and Didi had played golf at school and were rather good, but they were not above playing at less than their best so as not to put the gentlemen's pride out of joint. They knew how these things worked.

By the seventh hole, it was obvious that Freddy was a terrible golfer, and that Mr. Farrington was actually very good. Freddy looked as though he would gladly throw his entire club set into the water hazard.

When the eighteenth hole was complete, and they were headed back toward the clubhouse, the clouds transformed to a thick gray and a light rain began to fall.

"Perfect timing," commented Marcus, who had performed decently.

"Rather," said Charlie. "Would have been beastly if this had happened an hour ago."

Mr. Farrington had organized a lovely tea at the clubhouse, and they all settled in to eat a healthy amount of cake and biscuits as the rain now came down in sheets outside. The men talked of things that did not interest Dodo in the least, and she let her gaze wander to Mrs. Alexander who was sporting a very pretty, small, sapphire pendant. Dodo approved. Colonel Alexander was regarding his wife as one might look at a beloved puppy. It was rather sweet.

Octavia had chosen not to play, with the excuse that there was so much to do to get ready for the evening's activities. Dodo hoped very much that she was not sleeping off a drunken stupor.

She had known the Farringtons for years and had never noticed this vice before. She wondered what might have happened that Octavia wished to escape.

"I think you might have found your sport," Julian whispered close to her ear. "You made remarkable progress. I'd be happy to tutor you if you like."

She turned and pursed her scarlet lips provocatively before saying, "I might just do that Mr. Jeffries."

Anita was looking at her watch again, and though she had played quite well, Dodo had the distinct impression that she would rather have been elsewhere. At present, she was not engaging in the conversation around her at all.

Didi was chatting companionably with Charlie. "I love the horses," Dodo heard her say.

"The races?" interrupted Marcus who was sitting next to Didi again. "Love a day at the races, myself."

Didi turned slightly so that her back was now to Marcus. "Of course, Daddy owns a couple of thoroughbreds, so we always go to see them run."

"Is that so?" responded Charlie. "I'll have to look out for those."

"Won fifty pounds last month," said Marcus to no one.

Didi looked over at Dodo and rolled her baby-blue eyes.

When they were all full to bursting of cake, they motored back to Farrington Hall to get ready for dinner and charades. Octavia was nowhere to be found.

Lizzie, who had arrived during dinner the night before, had drawn them both a bath and they each retired to their own bathrooms to soak. Luxury.

Dodo sank into the warmth of the rose water and laid her head against the bathtub. The silky liquid caressed her skin as the plumes of steam curled into the air like sprites. She smiled as she remembered how she and Didi had pretended to be beginners to soothe the males' egos. She breathed in with satisfaction at the memory of Julian's hand on hers as she swung her club. As the pleasant sensations rolled on, the calm was suddenly pierced by a blood-curdling scream. Dodo sat bolt upright, reached for a towel, and jumped out of the bath. Padding across the tile floor, she wrapped the towel around her and poked her head out of the door. Other heads were popped out all along the corridor as an unusually harried Mrs. Alexander ran out of her room crying, "Call the police! Call the police! Oh my, that piece is absolutely priceless. What to do, what to do?"

As if Dodo were watching an act in a play, Mr. Farrington rushed up to the landing, running past the inquisitive guests. "My dear, what has happened?"

"Oh, Richard, the emerald necklace—it's been stolen!"

Chapter 7

"When did you last have it?" asked the tall, lean man in a gray trench coat, as Dodo slipped into the sitting room. She could not resist a mystery. She had dressed in record time so that she might eavesdrop on the activities surrounding the alleged theft. She assumed the man to be the local inspector. He looked to be in his early thirties and wore his face clean shaven—a ruggedly handsome face that bore signs of fatigue. Under the proverbial raincoat he wore a wrinkled brown suit, an indication that there was no Mrs. Inspector. Sitting on a hard chair with a notebook and pencil, he was asking questions of Anne whose face was a study in agony.

"I wore it last night for dinner and dancing and then I put it on the dressing table opposite the bed by the window. I was so tired that I did not immediately put it into my portable safe," she explained. "I meant to put it in the safe when I woke up, but I slept late and was in rather a hurry to get ready for our golfing expedition."

"And it was gone when you returned." He glanced at Dodo, eyebrows raised, and she flashed a smile in response. He returned to his notebook, a slight pink infusing his cheeks.

"Yes," said Anne Alexander. "One of the staff must have taken it!"

"What makes you say that?" asked the inspector calmly.

"Well, what other explanation can there be?"

"Unless you have evidence to suggest that it was a maid, we cannot accuse anyone," he replied. "Now, how did you realize it was missing?"

"I was deciding what to wear this evening before taking a bath. In reaching to take off my pendant, I remembered that I had forgotten to put my emerald necklace away. I walked over to the dressing table to place it and the pendant in the safe when I saw that it was gone. I called the maid up—I'm using one of Mrs. Farrington's as we left ours at home—and asked her if she had seen the necklace when she came in to get me ready this morning.

She is rather a vacant girl and asked me to describe the necklace—she had helped me put it on the night before—and remembering, said that now that I mentioned it, she hadn't and assumed that I had put it into the safe."

"What time did you leave your room for golfing?"

"Well, I went down for a quick breakfast at nine-thirty and ran back up to get a scarf for the outing. I do not remember seeing it then but really, Inspector, I wasn't paying attention."

"And what time did you return?" said the inspector, shrugging out of his raincoat and smoothing his rather rumpled tie.

"It must have been around five as we had tea at the club and then came back to get ready for dinner."

"Did you lock your room while you were gone?"

"Of course not! I am with friends." Anne looked scandalized.

"But you brought a safe?" The irony was not lost on Anne. She colored.

"I don't wish my jewels to be a temptation, Inspector. There are servants and tradesman in big country houses and it just seems prudent to keep valuables locked away and out of sight."

"Indeed, ma'am. So, the room was unlocked between ten o' clock this morning and five this afternoon and anyone could have gone in and taken the necklace?"

"But the maid did not recall seeing it when she came to dress Mrs. Alexander at nine," interrupted Dodo. "Therefore, it is possible that it was already gone."

"And who are you, if I may ask?" The inspector dropped the notebook to his side momentarily.

Dodo thrust out a hand. "Lady Dorothea Dorchester. How do you do?"

"The Lady Dorothea who discovered the saboteur of the prize racehorse?" he exclaimed.

"One and the same." She bobbled her head slightly, gratified that he knew of her sleuthing.

"That is a good observation Lady Dorothea. I will be talking to the maid directly, pinpointing times and assessing her observations," assured the inspector. He turned back to Anne

Alexander. "Did anyone know that you planned to bring the jewels this weekend?"

"No. Well, yes. I mentioned it to Mrs. Farrington a few days ago. Octavia is a close friend and I wanted to show it to her as it is a newish piece and she had not seen it yet. But no one else knew."

At that moment Octavia pushed through the door and rushed over to Anne, grasping her hands and exclaiming, "Oh my dear, what an absolutely awful thing! I do hope it is just lost or mislaid. I cannot believe that any of our staff would ever, ever stoop to theft!" As she turned away from Anne to sit, Dodo noticed that her make-up had smudged, and her hair was slightly messy.

The inspector cleared his throat. The two older women turned their faces to him.

"Has it occurred to you that it could have been one of the guests?"

Two javelins could not have pinned the inspector with greater success than the dagger looks Octavia and Anne cast at him. Dodo hid a grin at his faux pas with her hand. "Good grief, Inspector!" cried Octavia, "Do you appreciate the caliber of the people we have staying here? I reject your suggestion out of hand! It must be one of the staff, though I cannot believe it, or a passing thief."

The inspector sucked in his cheeks before continuing. "Was your window open while you were golfing, Mrs. Alexander?"

Anne Alexander frowned and putting her hand to her neck, looked at her husband. "I'm not sure…Arthur, do you recall?"

Dodo looked over at the Colonel who had been incredibly quiet and looked rather green and shocked. *Surely, the jewels were insured.*

"Ahh, let me think." He scratched his chin. "No, I don't think so…"

"Was your room cold and damp when you came back from golf? It had rained while we were gone and if the window had been open…" Dodo let the question hang.

"Oh, you're right," Anne agreed "I would have gone straight to close the window if it had been open. No, it must have been closed."

"Then how do you suggest a thief might have entered your room?" said the inspector carefully. "I doubt they came through the front door in broad daylight, and I understand that Mrs. Farrington stayed home."

Everyone looked at Octavia who flushed red and stammered, "Yes...yes...I was here."

"Thieves are, by definition, devious, are they not, Inspector?" countered Mrs. Alexander. "He will have found some way in I suppose."

The inspector wore a very patient look and closed his notebook.

"Mrs. Farrington," he said, addressing Octavia, "I will need to talk to all the staff and particularly to the maid assigned to Mrs. Alexander. I have directed my constables to do a thorough examination of the room to ensure that the necklace did not fall down a crevice. They will also dust for fingerprints."

"Of course, of course, Inspector," said Octavia, struggling to her feet to lead the inspector from the room.

"What an insolent fellow!" cried Anne as soon as he left. "Fancy suggesting that it could be a guest? He has no understanding of the upper classes, obviously!"

Dodo suppressed a smirk. How arrogant her class of people were. An outsider such as the inspector would have no idea how to handle them. She saw this as her opening to suggest helping him – an insider's view. He was unlikely to get much helpful information out of the guests if he continued to blunder in like a bull in a china shop. She would offer to facilitate the investigation. She had experience in her resume after all, having helped with such investigations at school and last year, as the inspector had noted, when her father's racehorse had been sabotaged. She glided from the room to follow the inspector.

***

Agnes Brown was as plain as her name. She had mousey brown, limp hair, a round, thick face and small, dark eyes. But her expression was eager and excited.

Strange, given the circumstances.

Dodo had approached the inspector in the passageway to plead her case regarding interviewing the guests by reciting her past experience and even giving him a reference for one Inspector Dowd. She declared that he was welcome to search her room first if necessary. Though reluctant at first, he happened to know the inspector which laid to rest many of his initial doubts.

"My sergeant has the flu, so I am down a man," he mused. "Alright then, but I'm in charge."

"Of course you are, Inspector."

Having succeeded thus far she had then persuaded him that having her present with the young female staff particularly, might put them at their ease.

"I don't see that it would do any harm," he agreed which was how she found herself witnessing the interview with Agnes in the servant's area.

As the inspector invited Agnes to sit down at the servant's table, she was positively euphoric. She leaned forward eagerly, mouth slightly open, her breathing rapid.

The inspector opened his little notebook and pencil.

"You are aware that a necklace of great value has gone missing, Miss Brown?"

"Ooooh yes!" she exclaimed. "We heard the barney all the way downstairs."

"I understand that you helped Mrs. Alexander put the necklace on and then take it off on Thursday evening. Is that correct?"

"Actually, since their party went late, she sent a message down to say that she did not need help undressing after the dancing, so I went to bed."

"But you did help her put it on?"

"Yes."

"And what did you think of it?"

"Well, it was a bit showy for my taste, you know, but it sparkled something lovely." Her quick eyes glittered at the memory.

"Was it very heavy?"

"Yes. The stones were so big. I remember wondering if it would make her neck ache."

"Do you know how much it is worth?"

"A packet I'd say, but I don't know exactly, no." Her fingers crept onto the table, not in anxiety but in anticipation. Agnes Brown was clearly basking in all the attention, seemingly with little idea that she was under suspicion.

"You came to dress Mrs. Alexander the next morning. Did you notice the necklace on the dressing table?"

Agnes looked up at the ceiling making a show of trying to remember. "I don't think so."

"Did you expect to see it?"

"No. Mrs. Alexander had a portable safe that she used for her jewels. I suppose I assumed it was back in the safe."

"Did you take the necklace out of the safe the night before?"

"Crikey no! Mrs. Alexander did that and made sure to cover the lock so I wouldn't see the combination."

"To be clear then, the only time you saw the necklace was when you put it on Mrs. Alexander Thursday evening, before dinner, and you have not seen it since."

Agnes paused for dramatic effect. "Yes."

"Did you enter Mrs. Alexander's room after you helped her dress this morning and before she came back from the golf outing?"

Agnes flicked her eyes over to Dodo, then looked down before staring straight into the inspector's eyes. "No. I have other duties and I was helping get things ready for this evening's game of charades."

"Do you know of any other servant that was on the upper level during the day?"

"Well, there was Maisie who makes the beds. She had to do that late because the Colonel and his wife slept in -" she stopped abruptly. "You're not thinking it was Maisie that took it, are you? She's a good girl and would never!"

"No one is being accused of anything at the moment," said the inspector calmly, which was a white lie as Mrs. Alexander was sure it was one of the staff. "We are just trying to establish the last time the necklace was seen and where everyone was."

Agnes took on an injured look and brushed invisible dust from her uniform. "That's okay then," she murmured.

"You are free to go, Miss Brown, but I may need to question you further in the future."

Agnes stood and bobbed a curtsey before leaving the room.

"What do you think?" asked the inspector. "Do you believe her, Miss Dorchester?"

Delighted that he would ask her opinion, Dodo clasped her hands on the table. "Well, since you ask, I do think she was holding something back." She engaged his eye. "Why? Did you have the same impression?"

"I had the curious feeling she was…strategizing…as she was answering our questions," he said.

"You mean when you asked her if she had been into the bedroom this afternoon? Yes, I felt that she was editing what she was telling you, as she was talking. So, it is quite possible that she slipped up there while Mrs. Alexander was out…or saw something. What will you do?"

"I'll have my men search the servant's quarters. Tell them it's standard operating procedure. I'll search *all* the rooms so as not to raise suspicions."

Ironically, Dodo felt that the inspector was editing *his* comments to *her*. She was sure there was more going on in his mind than he let on. But why should he tell her everything? Or anything really? The inspector did not know her personally and did not owe her anything. Perhaps she could do something to gain his confidence and prove her worth.

"I could ask my maid, Lizzie, to keep her ears open below stairs," Dodo suggested.

The handsome inspector scratched his head and seemed to deliberate. "*That* would be most helpful Miss Dorchester." Then he turned a rather devastating smile on her. "Assuming, of course, your maid is not the thief?" *Was he flirting?*

They were interrupted by a timid knock on the door.

"Come in!" bellowed the inspector. The door crept open, revealing a chit of a girl in a housemaid's uniform, trembling in the doorway.

Maisie Briggs could not have been more than fifteen. She was skinny and short and had bucked front teeth. The inspector modified his tone. "Please, come in," he said.

Maisie's eyes darted left and right as she moved toward the proffered seat and sat down as though the chair might swallow her.

"Now, Miss Briggs-"

"I ain't no thief!" she blurted out, highly strung and ready to cry at the least provocation.

"We are not suggesting that you are," continued the inspector in an even softer tone, "we are merely trying to ascertain when the jewels were last seen."

Maisie wiped her nose with her sleeve and sniffed, nodding.

"I understand that you went up to make the bed in the Anderson's room while they were on the golfing expedition. Is that correct?"

Eyes big with fear, she nodded.

"And was the necklace on the dressing table when you entered?"

Again, the frightened eyes darted right and left. "No."

"No? Are you sure?" His tone had become sharp again, and Maisie shrank into the chair. He modified his intonation when he spoke next, his voice lighter. "Perhaps you would be more comfortable if Lady Dorothea asked you the questions?"

Maisie nodded mutely.

Elated at this course of events, Dodo quickly assessed the situation and moved closer to the frightened girl.

"Now, Maisie, there's no need to be frightened. You are not being accused of anything. Think hard. Can you remember if the necklace was there?"

Maisie closed her eyes. "No, it for sure weren't there. I went over to the dressing table to dust before I made up the bed." She opened her eyes. "Agnes had told us all about them emeralds. She said she had never seen anything so expensive in all her life. If they had been on the table, I would have admired them. They weren't there."

"Thank you, Maisie. Is there anything else you *do* remember that might be helpful to the inspector?"

Maisie flicked her eyes over to the inspector for an instant and settled them back onto Dodo's.

"I don't think so," she whispered.

"Did you see anyone else on the upper floor near the room while you were there?" she persisted.

"No, ma'am. The house was quiet as all the guests had gone to play golf and Mrs. Farrington was napping—" She stopped abruptly and glanced at the inspector again, her cheeks burning. "Oops, I shouldn't have said that. Everyone knows it but we're not supposed to talk about it. Please don't write that in your book."

"I don't see that it has any relevance to the case, do you Inspector?" assured Dodo.

"Not to worry. I won't put any notes about that," the inspector agreed.

"Thank you," Maisie said sincerely. "With the mistress…unavailable…we took a little break in the servant's yard all together and then started on our duties for the evening. We were all together for the whole afternoon until Mr. Farrington and the guests returned."

The inspector scribbled with his pencil.

"Can you think of any more questions?" he asked Dodo. She shook her head.

"Thank you, Maisie. You are free to go," he said.

In contrast to her entrance, Maisie was gone in a split second.

"Nothing useful there in my opinion," the inspector said.

"I agree. There was nothing to see as all the guests were gone and the servants are each other's alibis."

"Of course, they could all be in it together," he mused, with a twinkle in his eye. Dodo rolled her eyes.

The inspector looked at his watch. "I think I'll go and see if my constables have found anything and help to search the servant's rooms – and yours - " he winked, "before calling it a night. If you could talk to your maid…" He stood and handed her a card with his name and phone number on it. *Inspector Hornby*.

"I expect you will check with the local fences to see if they have received any stolen goods today," said Dodo, her scarlet nail tapping the card.

The inspector's head snapped back to her and a wry grin spread over his face. "You know what a 'fence' is Lady Dorothea?"

"Of course! Do you think I stay at home all day and sew needlepoint? It's a brave new world, Inspector!"

Inspector Hornby chuckled and his rugged face softened. "Indeed. Yes, I'll check with my sources to see if the necklace is being offered for sale." He reached for the handle to the door and tipped his hat. "Good day Lady Dorothea."

Chapter 8

"You think he was flirting?" queried Didi, her lip curling in curious disbelief as Dodo applied her makeup at the antique dressing table in her room.

"Of all the things I just told you, that is the one that stands out?" said Dodo wryly.

"Well, he is rather dishy for a police inspector," said Didi.

"Trust you to notice that when there's been a calamity." She applied some crimson lipstick, laughing.

"So, you think Agnes knew more than she was saying?" Didi's brow was knit as she came to sit on her sister's bed.

"I do. She took too long to answer and looked around the room to give herself time to think. You don't need time to think if you're telling the whole truth."

"True. When I smashed Ma's Ming vase with my tennis racquet, that's how Father knew it was me. I took too long to mount my defense. I got in terrible trouble for that—do you remember?"

"Focusing on the matter at hand," said Dodo with a grin, touching her cheek with some powder. "It certainly indicates that Agnes knows more."

"Do you think she actually stole the necklace?"

"No. It was rather bulky, not something you could just slip in your pocket. Do I think she is capable of stealing? Yes. She did not ooze honesty. Had it been the beautiful pendant Anne Alexander wore today, I might suspect Agnes. She is clearly fascinated with shiny things – as are most women. But no. Not this particular item. And what would she *do* with it? She could hardly wear it and if she tried to sell it, it would garner too much attention."

"So, what are you saying? That she might have seen who did?" squealed Didi.

"Perhaps. I've asked Lizzie to keep her ears open for gossip downstairs. That might give us a lead."

"Why didn't the inspector interview the guests yet, do you think?"

"I believe that if he doesn't find anything in the servants' rooms that he will turn his attention to us. However, I would bet ten thousand pounds that there is a constable stationed at the end of the driveway to see if any of us leave tonight."

***

Dinner that night was a subdued affair. The Alexanders took theirs in their room and Freddy was upstairs with a toothache, they were told. No one else felt inclined to be cheerful under the circumstances. Charades was canceled and everyone gathered in the sitting room after dinner chatting quietly.

Julian inevitably found his way onto a couch next to Dodo, in an alcove. She was secretly pleased. "Dashed business this," he said. "What do you think of it all?"

"It's a pretty daring crime. Such a large, extravagant piece. It took some nerve to carry out with the house full of people. Furthermore, no one really knew Anne was bringing it, which seems to rule out a random thief from outside the house. It suggests the theft was committed on impulse."

"By Jove!" Julian chortled. "You have given this some thought. I haven't considered further than how it affects me, to be honest."

"I do have a little experience with this kind of thing," she replied, running her finger around the top of her glass. "I used to help with this kind of thing at school. And last year I helped my father discover who sabotaged his racehorse. I seem to have a knack for detecting."

"Do you now? I didn't have you down as a gumshoe!"

She lifted her elegant foot, displaying a white, leather, high heel with a slim ankle strap, decorated with a glittering diamante buckle, which made Julian laugh. The whole room looked toward them as if he had made a loud noise at the library. "Oops." He lowered his voice. "A crime of opportunity then. If it was too bulky for the staff ..." he broke off considering. "I say, you seem to be suggesting that it was one of us. Who here would need to steal such an object? Our pedigree is well known."

She noticed his cheeks pale.

"Are you really so naïve as to still believe that everyone is as they appear? I know of several Dukes who are desperate for money these days. And what about the people who steal for the thrill?"

"Do such people exist?"

"I can assure you they do. Perhaps you do not remember the case of Lady Mountjoy who stole several bottles of perfume from *Harrod's*? She certainly could have afforded them, but it was more exciting to *steal* them. Kleptomania is the proper name for it. It was all hushed up by her husband and settled out of court, but I heard about it through the grapevine."

Julian raised his brow and smirked. "I was wrong about you," he said. "I thought you were some sheltered debutante, but I see I am mistaken."

Dodo touched his arm and whispered in his ear. "How about some fun? Let's make up stories about all the people in the room, giving each person a motive." She slipped her arm through his and inched closer. "Let's begin with Marcus. He went to Monaco and put ten thousand pounds on black…"

"And he won," said Julian, warming to the game, "but then in a moment of madness he put everything on red—"

"And lost it all!" finished Dodo with a flourish.

"All right, how about Anita?"

"Hmmm. I say she fell in love with a Spanish Duke, who turned out to be a con man and stole all her money!"

"You are a little too good at this!" declared Julian, his shoulders stiffening. "What about Charlie? I suggest that he bought a racehorse for an outrageous amount of money, and it died of a fever a week later. Calamitous timing, as he had procrastinated getting insurance for it!"

"Bravo!" said Dodo.

"Now do me," he said, holding her hand up and lacing his fingers through hers. She took a cleansing breath and struck an attitude of concentration. "I say, you invested in a racecar and crashed it, causing your investors to get cold feet." As she spoke, she was surprised to see his handsome face freeze, the color drain and his hand withdraw ever so slightly. She laughed nervously. "Dead on I suppose," she said, worried that her scenario had hit a little close to home.

He cleared his throat and fixed a phony smile on his face. "Haha, yes. Absolutely spot on!" His voice carried a stiff tenor.

"Shall I go and get us a drink?" she asked, hoping that by leaving she would sever the sudden awkwardness that had sprung up between them.

"Yes, please." Julian rubbed his nose with his knuckle.

She hurried over to the sideboard and poured them both a drink, allowing him time to pull himself together.

As she glanced back, she was shocked by the grimace that had replaced the fake smile.

What is the real story?

***

"So, the servants are buzzing about being suspected?" asked Dodo as Lizzie helped her undress and get ready for bed. Lizzie had been her maid since she was fourteen and had become more of a trusted friend than a mere servant.

"Yes. Poor Maisie was almost in tears after her interview with you and the inspector. Mrs. Granger, the cook, had to give her sweet tea and a biscuit to calm her. Maisie kept repeating that she was a good girl and Mrs. Granger kept telling her that she wasn't under suspicion.

Agnes, on the other hand, was boasting about not being nervous at all under the inspector's scrutiny. Then she said something you might find interesting m'lady. She said the inspector wasn't as clever as he thought, and that she knew things that no one else knows."

Dodo remembered the impression she'd had that Agnes was holding something back. "Did she say what those things were?"

"Mrs. Granger asked her right out and she said that she was keeping it to herself but that it might prove valuable."

"Oh dear. I hope she doesn't go around saying that. It could be dangerous." Dodo wiped the scarlet lipstick from her lips and smoothed cold cream over her face and neck.

"Did you believe her, Lizzie, or do you think she was just enjoying the attention?"

"She does seem like a girl who looks for ways to get the limelight, but I'm not sure, m'lady. I'm afraid I don't know her well enough."

"Well, what you have told me is invaluable, Lizzie. Well done! However, I am fearful for the girl. It is never wise to boast about such things. I think you should warn her that she is playing a dangerous game and that if she has any information, she would do well to tell it to the inspector."

"Will do, m'lady."

After Lizzie left, Dodo went into her sister's room.

Didi had already jumped into bed and groaned at the interruption. "A girl needs her beauty sleep!"

"Yes, you need a lot," Dodo joked which elicited a pillow thrown at her. "I was just talking to Lizzie and she said that Agnes the maid is boasting that she knows something relevant to the case that she did not tell the inspector. Something that could prove valuable."

Didi sat up. "Goodness! Did she give a hint as to what she meant?"

"No, and Lizzie isn't even sure if she is telling the truth or just seeking attention."

Didi propped herself up on one elbow as Dodo sat on the end of her bed. "I hope she doesn't live to regret that."

"I had the same thought."

Chapter 9

Inspector Hornby had asked everyone to stay on at Farrington Hall in case he should feel the need to interview them, and the atmosphere had become horribly strained. Everyone opted to take breakfast in their rooms, except Dodo who was finding the whole thing rather fun. Other than when she was working with fashion, she was never happier than when she had a good mystery to solve.

The other guests mostly all ventured downstairs for lunch, however, and to everyone's relief, Octavia announced that they would go ahead with the croquet and afternoon tea as planned. The change in the room was palpable—Dodo felt as though a heavy chain had been thrown from everyone. Natural conversation resumed with Mr. Farrington sharing the latest cricket scores and Octavia reading aloud from the society pages of the Times.

"I would have dressed differently had I known we would be playing," commented Didi, as lunch came to an end. She had chosen a rather tight-fitting skirt.

"Of course you would have, darlings," said Octavia "I'll give you plenty of time to change and then we can begin the game promptly at two o' clock."

Back in their rooms, Dodo rang the bell for Lizzie to come up. When she arrived, her eyes were brimming with news as she thrust open the door and burst into the room, arms flapping.

"Out with it then," said Dodo with a smile.

"Agnes showed up wearing silk stockings today. Real silk!" she crowed.

"Did she now?" said Dodo, biting her cheek in concentration.

"Now where did a maid get the money for something like that?" continued Lizzie.

"Exactly," agreed Dodo.

"Did you ask her?" said Didi.

"I complimented her on them and asked if they were a gift. She merely smiled and tapped her nose, indicating that it was a secret."

Dodo's face creased with concern. "Oh, my goodness, do you think she might be blackmailing someone? She's playing with fire if she is, silly girl!"

"Blackmail?" said Didi, "What do you mean?"

"When someone suddenly comes into money there has to be a reason. Imagine if Agnes knows who the thief is and told them she would keep quiet for some cash?"

"Oh, yes I see." Didi picked up the lipstick and smeared it on her own lips. "That would place the thief in a corner -"

" -and they might do something more drastic to keep her quiet," finished Dodo.

After Lizzie left, Didi threw her Brownie camera around her neck and pulled her white hat to a jaunty angle as she looked at her sister in the mirror. Dodo was wearing a chiffon, floral dress that hung loosely around the hips and sensible, but stylish sandals. "Silk stockings are very expensive," Didi commented. "Do you think *we* should mention it to the inspector?"

Dodo continued to put the finishing touches on her make-up before answering.

"Mrs. McCreedy, the housekeeper, seems to be an efficient, intelligent woman. If one of her maids suddenly shows up wearing silk stockings, I am sure the woman will mention it to the inspector herself."

"Yes, you're probably right," Didi answered languidly, touching her cheeks to check on her rouge. "You looked very cozy with Julian last night," she said, changing topics seamlessly.

"Mmm," replied Dodo, checking her ensemble in the long mirror. Their relationship had definitely shifted the night before and Dodo wasn't exactly sure where she stood with Julian now. It was obvious that something she said had affected him. She hoped the croquet game would help to unruffle his feathers. She felt as though she was falling for him and wanted to set things right.

"What does that mean?"

Dodo told her what had happened and Didi spun around. "You think you may have hit on a truth?"

"I don't know, but I have a feeling that if the inspector turns his sights on us, he is going to pull all sorts of skeletons out of the closet."

***

If Julian had been rattled the night before, he showed no signs of it during croquet - thankfully. He had skipped lunch but had arrived early for the game looking thoroughly delicious in cricket whites, which were a weakness of Dodo's and quite put the theft out of her mind. He approached her as she arrived on the back lawn, which had been set up with the hoops, and brought her a mallet.

"You are looking particularly lovely this afternoon," he crooned.

"Why thank you Mr. Jeffries. You look very dapper yourself."

The guests dribbled out in ones and twos. The Alexanders were last out – Dodo was surprised they came at all given the circumstances. Anne looked pale and her husband could not muster a smile.

"Now," said Octavia, when everyone had arrived, "let's divide up into teams of two…"

"We are already a team," remarked Julian as he put his arm possessively around Dodo.

Normally, Dodo would bristle at being manhandled in this way, but she was relieved that things weren't awkward between them and besides, she was rapidly succumbing to his charisma. She happily surrendered.

Marcus swiftly moved to Didi's side as she frowned, blowing her hair out of her eyes, and Charlie walked over to Anita leaving Freddy to pair up with his mother. Mr. Farrington was absent.

"How's the tooth, old man?" asked Charlie of Freddy.

"Much better, thanks. Got it taken care of this morning." His fingers went to his cheek as he spoke, "It's been bothering me for days."

"Now," continued Octavia, "let's throw a coin to see which team goes first."

Didi and Marcus won the toss and the game began. Croquet is a leisurely game and a table with fresh lemonade had been set up for couples who were not taking their turn. The sun was out, the sky was blue, and for a while everyone could forget that a terrible theft had occurred the day before. Everyone except the Alexanders, that is.

When Dodo was not playing, she enjoyed the sun, eyes closed, soaking in the warmth of the rays. Several other players followed her lead, letting some of the tension drain away.

"The weather is marvelous today, isn't it?" Julian said, as he came to sit by her after their turn.

"Mmm. Just what the doctor ordered," replied Dodo.

"I was thinking that after we all head home you might like to go to dinner or something?" he continued.

Dodo opened one eye and studied him. His expression was earnest, and her heart produced a little flutter.

"I would like that very much," she said, shading her eyes with her hand.

"We could take in a play or a dance club afterward," he pushed on, brushing her hand with his long fingers. She felt butterflies in her stomach.

"I love dancing," she replied.

"That's settled then." He linked their little fingers.

Didi sank onto a chair next to them. "I'm going to kill that man!" she whispered in a strangled voice.

"Who? Marcus?"

"Yes! He is such a pig. He keeps bossing me around and criticizing my strokes. He has the manners of a Neanderthal. I swear if he tells me how to swing one more time, I'm going to—"

"We get the idea," interrupted Dodo.

"Oh." Didi searched their faces. "Did I come at a bad time?"

"Not at all," said Julian with good manners. "I think it is just about our turn, Dodo."

He helped her up and she made a face at her sister who had the good graces to mouth, "Sorry."

Julian was not very good at the game, as it turned out, though he had a great style. Marcus surprised everyone with dead on accuracy through the hoops, winning the first round with Didi easily. It was a marvelously relaxing afternoon, just the ticket after the stress of the missing jewels and the arrival of the police.

"Super game, everyone," said Octavia, after the third round. "Let's all sit here under the shade of the oaks, and I'll alert the staff that we are ready for tea—" Her speech was interrupted by a distant, but blood curdling scream and everyone looked at each other in alarm.

"I'll go and see what that's all about," said Freddy, jumping up and running toward the house.

Octavia's face fell and she suddenly looked old and frightened. "Oh dear, oh dear. I hope nothing else has gone missing." She sat down on a white, iron chair heavily and put her hand to her chest, squinting her eyes as if in pain. Dodo came to her side and crouched down, squeezing her hand. Octavia opened her eyes, smiling in gratitude.

They all sat, silent and immobile, anxiously waiting for news from the house like actors waiting for the director, when Marcus spotted Freddy running toward them, scowling. They all looked in his direction, and as Freddy approached, he gasped for air.

"It's Agnes…" he exclaimed, "…she's dead."

Chapter 10

Dodo examined the inspector as he stood at the front of the room. His suit was more crumpled than the day before and stubble dotted his chin. The shadow emphasized his sculpted jaw. He had entered the room with little energy and now had his pad and pencil in hand, adrift. Murder, it would seem, was above his pay grade.

"Agnes Brown has been murdered by strangulation with a silk scarf," he stated.

Shock rippled around the room, and Anne Alexander failed to stifle a sob. Groans of disbelief emanated from the women as the men sat in somber silence.

"Do you believe this to be connected to the theft?" asked Octavia, her voice shaking.

"It is too early in our inquiries to draw such conclusions, but I would guess that we will find a connection." Octavia dug her face into her husband's shoulder. He had arrived amidst the initial hubbub of the discovery.

"Now, I know that this is all very distasteful, but the stakes have been raised," the inspector continued. "No one is permitted to leave, and I will need to interview everyone alone. Lady Dorothea, I wonder if you would consider assisting me with the interviews – after I first interview you of course – and if Mr. and Mrs. Farrington have no objections?" He turned his tired eyes to her. Dodo jerked with surprise and grabbed her necklace, looking around the room for any signs of confirmation from her friends, thrilled at the invitation.

"Not at all," murmured Mr. Farrington, "Her experience in such matters is well known to us."

"Unless there are any other objections?" the inspector continued, swinging his gaze around the room.

Surprisingly, Octavia grabbed Dodo's hand and squeezed. "Oh yes, this will be much less distasteful with a friendly advocate at hand. You understand us so much better," she whispered. "I fear the police will be so heavy-handed without a steadying influence."

"Alright then," said the inspector. "We are also awaiting the imminent arrival of Chief Inspector Blood of Scotland Yard. Murder is a very different matter than theft altogether, as you know, and he will be leading this investigation when he arrives." A hushed murmur rumbled through the anxious crowd. Dodo watched every face. Each one displayed apprehension and fear.

"Who will tell her parents?" gasped Octavia, suddenly. "I don't think I am up to the job, Inspector."

"Someone from the police force will perform that task, ma'am." He ran a hand down the back of his hair.

Octavia sniffed into a handkerchief.

"Mr. Farrington, is there a study that we can use to interview your guests?" continued the inspector.

Mr. Farrington looked up, dazed. His ruddy face pinched into a squint at the inspector's words. Finally, he said, "Yes, yes, of course. Please follow me."

"Lady Dorothea?" The inspector nodded in her direction, and she stood to leave the room.

Before they exited, the inspector added, "No one is to go up to their rooms at this point. The upper level is now a crime scene, and until the Chief Inspector has surveyed upstairs, that area will be out of bounds to everyone. The staff have been instructed to bring tea, but it may take a while as they are understandably in shock. You are free to go out into the garden or anywhere on this level, but no one is to leave the grounds." The occupants of the room nodded.

Dodo followed the inspector through the door, looking back to bestow a weak smile on Didi. Dodo had experienced several crimes recently, but her sister was still an innocent, and shock was stamped on her fragile features.

Mr. Farrington walked with heavy step to a room in the east wing, his broad shoulders hunched. The door was heavy oak and as they entered Dodo was blasted by the smell of pipe tobacco and leather. He walked over to his desk and pulled up a chair on the other side. "Will this do?"

"Yes, this will work very well, sir," said the inspector. "Do you mind if we move some of the other chairs?"

"No, no. Whatever you need."

There was a short knock at the door. "Come in!" barked Mr. Farrington, resuming some of his authority. A manservant entered and said, "A Chief Inspector Blood has arrived, sir and is waiting in the entrance hall."

"That was quick," said Inspector Hornby in wonder.

The three of them left the study and followed the servant to the vestibule where a very tall man in a raincoat had his broad back to them. He twirled around as he heard their footsteps and whisked off his hat. He was about thirty-five years old and simply oozed masculinity. Dodo halted, having expected someone much older and curmudgeonly. *Attractive.*

"Good evening, I am Chief Inspector Blood of Scotland Yard." He held out his hand and Mr. Farrington shook it. "I happened to be at a police station not far from here when I got the call," he said by way of explanation.

The chief inspector had a scratchy bass voice, rich brown eyes, and almost black, wavy hair. The effect was unnervingly pleasant.

Turning to Dodo he asked, "Mrs. Farrington?"

There was a lilt, indicating his surprise at her youth.

"No," clarified Inspector Hornby, "this is Lady Dorothea Dorchester. She is a guest here." The chief inspector's eyes scrunched with confusion. "Then why is she here?" he growled at Hornby with an air of belligerent impertinence. Indignation brewed and she felt heat rise to her face and a defense rush to her mouth. She may not be a police officer, but he could show a little more courtesy.

"Lady Dorothea has been very useful in helping me interview the staff, particularly the women, concerning the theft," explained the inspector. Chief Inspector Blood glared at her and she held his stare with defiance. "A *civilian* has been helping you with the investigation?" demanded the chief inspector

Impudent man!

Inspector Hornby held up his hand in a sign of peace. "I happened to have previous knowledge that Lady Dorothea has helped the police in several cases and has proven to be an intelligent and valuable asset, sir. In addition, she is privy to certain conversations of the guests that may elicit clues, and she has a maid who is gathering information from below stairs."

The chief inspector continued his glare, nostrils flaring. Dodo stepped forward and held out her hand. Chief Inspector Blood looked at it but instead of shaking it, addressed the inspector. "Hornby, this is *most* irregular!" Dodo let her hand fall slowly to her side, bristling with indignation. The man had absolutely no manners.

However, she was not wet behind the ears. If she wanted to participate in this investigation, which she did, she would have to control her temper. Lashing out, though he deserved it, would damage her chances. The lure of the mystery stopped her tongue.

Inspector Hornby glanced at her apologetically before saying, "I have found her to be a very worthy assistant, sir. Perhaps you could give her a chance?"

Chief Inspector Blood waited, looking her up and down as if she were a cow for sale at auction. She felt a wave of humiliation crash within her and dislike swell.

Intolerable man!

Finally, the chief inspector harrumphed and pushed past them toward the stairs. "Show me the crime scene!"

Dodo hung back at the bottom for a moment, since he had not given permission for her to be involved. However, curiosity beat out mortification and she climbed the stairs softly like a cat so as not to attract attention to herself.

At the top, she crept along the hallway to the corner and peeked around. There laying with her legs in a most unnatural position, was poor Agnes staring straight at her. The eyes were glazed and empty and her tongue protruded slightly. Dodo could not stop a small gasp escaping. It was true that she had helped solve crimes before, but this was the first murder victim she had witnessed. Nausea crested like a geyser, and she shrank back around the corner taking deep breaths to steady herself.

Once she had gained control over her faculties, Dodo risked another look, avoiding a connection with the girl's dead face. Agnes was lying just outside the Alexander's room, the door of which was open, and a floral, silk scarf was lying beside her. She wore her maid's uniform which had risen slightly, exposing the expensive silk stockings Lizzie had mentioned.

The chief inspector was examining every detail of Agnes, consumed. Without warning he dropped to the floor, cheek pressed against the carpet, inspecting the hallway. Dodo disappeared like lightning back around the corner but alas, not before he had seen her. He let out a loud sigh of exasperation.

She squeezed her eyes shut and wrinkled her nose.

Thinking it prudent to return to the drawing room, she descended the stairs and opened the door. The hum of voices paused, but on seeing that it was her, the buzzing resumed in the form of questions. She held up her hands in surrender. "I have been dismissed," she said.

"Dismissed?" said Mr. Farrington.

"Chief Inspector Blood does not appreciate my talents," she said, crossing her legs.

"Can you tell us anything?" asked Octavia.

"I can tell you that the chief inspector is a pig of a man," she said, rearranging her necklace.

"Oh, that seems harsh," said Didi.

"Yes, but I did manage to see the crime scene," she continued.

Everyone stopped talking.

"I have seen the body of poor Agnes. Such a senseless waste of a life."

Octavia could not control herself and erupted in tears as her husband did his best to console her.

Didi ran up to Dodo. "Isn't this just awful," she whispered, hoarsely, "but you guessed something like this might happen, didn't you?"

"I thought Agnes would be unwise to blackmail a thief, if that was how she came by the silk stockings, but I never suspected that the thief would *murder* her!"

Julian approached, and the two sisters swiftly ended their conversation. "This is rather terrible, what? Do you think we will all have to stay beyond tomorrow? There are people I will need to tell; plans I will have to change. Did the police say anything?"

"No," Dodo said, quietly, unnerved that Julian was anxious to leave. He grabbed her hand and brushed his thumb over her knuckles. The tender act did little to erase the heavy emotions. She slipped her hand out of his.

"Though the thought of spending more time with *you* is rather appealing, a chap has things to attend to." His jaw was clenched.

"Murder changes everything," she snapped. "You can ask the police about it when they interview you."

Stepping back, he shoved a hand through his hair and went to fix himself a drink.

Dodo looked around the room. Anne Alexander was also in tears and looked done in, as her husband comforted her with soothing clichés. Octavia gave the impression that she might faint and was fanning herself wildly while Mr. Farrington's face was lined and troubled. Freddy was talking nineteen to the dozen with Charlie and Anita, who kept looking at her watch. What was it about the time that occupied her so much?

Marcus was the only person in the room who seemed relaxed. He was nursing a whiskey, legs crossed, watching Didi like a lovesick puppy as though no murder had occurred at all. Everyone else was clearly on edge.

Was one of these people a murderer? It seemed impossible since they had all been outside together – all except Mr. Farrington. She looked at the man she had known all her life trying to cast him in the role of killer. Instead he showed every sign of bewilderment and concern. Looking around the room again she tried to remember if anyone had gone inside the house during play. Her memory failed her. The only innocents she was sure of were herself and Didi. Everyone else had to be a suspect no matter how uncomfortable the thought made her.

Chapter 11

The chief inspector was glaring at her as she sat across the desk from him. "Well?" he spat.

Determined to punish the disrespectful man by delaying her answer as long as possible, Dodo narrowed her eyes, swung her hair and examined her nails. "I was out on the lawn the entire time we were playing croquet, Chief Inspector," she said eventually, drumming up her most aristocratic pronunciation.

She believed that Chief Inspector Blood had reluctantly allowed himself to be persuaded by Inspector Hornby to permit her to remain during the interviews. That it was against his better instincts was evident by his tone and the pulse in the vein on his temple. She was therefore the first to be interviewed. Again.

A knock on the door interrupted the interview. A young constable entered and handed the chief inspector a note. As he read it, Dodo watched his expression change. He turned to Inspector Hornby. "After questioning the staff, we can confirm that Agnes Brown was alive after the croquet began, and everyone but Agnes remained in the kitchen area until Maisie's cry went up."

"Well, that gives me a solid alibi, doesn't it, Chief Inspector?" Dodo grinned.

He mumbled something into his collar and then louder said, "And tell me about the other guests. Did anyone leave at any time?"

"I have been asking myself the same question, Chief Inspector." She closed her eyes, trying to wring out the memories from her mind. She saw Octavia leaning back, soaking up the sun in a wrought iron chair, the Alexanders playing the game half-heartedly, Marcus and Didi a team, hitting the ball straight and true, Charlie sitting on a bench with Anita, and Freddy missing the hoops by a mile. Everyone was present in the tableau in her mind, but the game had lasted a long time and she had spent a lot of that time with her eyes closed, basking in the sun. She could not be sure.

She opened her eyes and was startled to see the chief inspector staring at her intensely. He coughed, averting his eyes quickly.

"No, I'm sorry. I cannot remember anyone leaving, but then we were all trying to forget that a theft had occurred and the ugly truth that we were all considered suspects." She folded her arms and fiddled with her diamond earring. "Not much of a witness, am I?" Then she remembered the thoughts that had come to her in the sitting room that might be relevant.

"Mr. Farrington was not there for the game at all. I am not for one minute suggesting that he had anything to do with this, but it is a fact. I think he went to have a golf club mended. He arrived after the body was discovered. As for everyone else, I'm afraid that I was concentrating on the game and didn't notice what they were doing. If anyone left during play, I did not notice."

"Hmmph!" growled Chief Inspector Blood. "And everyone could vouch that you never left, I suppose?"

"Absolutely, Chief Inspector, because it is the truth!" Dodo crossed her arms and held the chief inspector's gaze.

"Well, it appears that *someone* left and went to the house. Hopefully, there are more observant witnesses among the other guests." He sighed with disdain, closing his eyes as if in pain.

"Chief Inspector," Dodo began, feeling her exasperation reach desperate levels. "If my presence here is so distasteful to you, why are you letting me stay?" She cast a quick glance at Inspector Hornby who had remained diplomatically silent through the whole exchange, though his eyes were twinkling.

Chief inspector Blood colored slightly, fingered his tie, and while lowering his voice, growled, "Sir Matthew Cusworth, Chief Commander of Police, called me on the telephone to advise me to involve you. He is aware of your skills in these, uh, matters and feels that your presence will help facilitate my inquiries with the…upper classes." Every word had been an effort, and his voice had been so low that she had almost missed the recommendation. It was too tempting to annoy this brusque man and she leaned forward, enjoying the chance to revel in his obvious discomfort. "I'm sorry Inspector, I missed that. What did you say?"

She risked another look at Inspector Hornby who was failing to hide a grin.

"I said," Chief Inspector Blood said a little more loudly, but just as frostily, "that Sir Matthew Cusworth, my superior, has recommended you. I gather he has been impressed with your work in the past." He looked up, glowering. "And it's *Chief Inspector*."

"Oh yes, how silly of me." She laughed. "*Chief Inspector*."

The chief inspector rustled some papers on the desk and cleared his throat. "Now, have you noticed anyone acting suspiciously during the rest of the weekend?" he continued.

"Well," she began, pushing her sable hair behind her ear, "actually, yes. Anita Anderson is very interested in the time. Very. She looks at her watch a hundred times a day. It's odd."

"Hmm," said the chief inspector writing down notes in his little brown book.

She hesitated, fighting the feeling of being disloyal but realizing that in a murder inquiry everything had the potential to be significant. "Julian Jeffries became rather agitated when I mentioned a hypothetical car accident during a silly game. I have no idea what *that* was about, but it left me feeling disconcerted. And then there is Marcus Makepeace. He is just an odd fish. Always has been. He is far too relaxed about the whole business." The chief inspector continued to scribble in his book.

"How well did you know the deceased?" The abrupt change of topic threw her off her guard momentarily.

"Not at all, I'm afraid. I brought my own maid. Lizzie."

"What did your maid think of Agnes Brown?"

"Agnes?" she said, chewing a scarlet lip. "After the theft, Inspector Hornby asked me to instruct Lizzie to keep her ear to the ground. The staff were the prime suspects. Lizzie told us that Agnes was an indiscreet gossip who loved being the center of attention."

He wrote some more, and Dodo leaned forward, tapping her long nails on the desk. "I am sure that you noticed the dead girl was wearing very expensive silk stockings, Chief Inspector?" He nodded, unimpressed. "Much too expensive for a maid to afford," she continued undeterred, "I believe she may have been blackmailing the thief." She ended with a flourish and sent a furtive wink to Inspector Hornby.

"Do you, now?" Chief Inspector Blood finally looked up and for the first time appeared to weigh her suggestion. "You believe that rather than being the thief herself, she may have witnessed the theft, and started blackmailing the culprit? Dangerous. What do you think Hornby? You talked to her."

"I think it is a rational theory. She was definitely hiding something when we interviewed her after the theft and she certainly liked the limelight."

"She wasn't particularly bright," added Dodo, "and according to Lizzie she made some suggestive statements at dinner about coming into money. She even talked about having enough funds to quit her job and hire a maid of her own. No one took her seriously at the time, of course, but if she were blackmailing someone…well, I don't think she would have realized the danger."

The pencil the chief inspector was using found its way to his mouth, and he chewed it pensively. She was reminded of Clark Gable. "It's possible," he finally admitted.

Inspector Hornby winked back at her.

"Let's get your sister in here, Miss Dorchester."

The chief inspector nodded to Inspector Hornby who opened the door and sent a waiting constable to retrieve Didi.

"Before she arrives, I want to set some ground rules," said the chief inspector, ominously.

"Of course." Dodo sat up straight and gave the chief inspector her full attention, blinking her sapphire eyes expectantly.

"You will sit over here." He pointed to a seat to the side and slightly behind he and Inspector Hornby. "And you will only enter the conversation if I invite you. Is that clear?"

"Crystal!" she said, flashing him her best smile.

His mouth lost its rigid line and he appeared to thaw a little.

"Yes, well…move over here then," said the chief inspector, straightening his tie.

They heard a light knock on the door and then the blond head of Didi bent into the room.

"Come in," said the chief inspector "Please sit down."

Dodo caught Didi's eye and threw her a small, nervous grin. Didi sat primly on the edge of her seat, clearly uncomfortable.

"Your name is Lady Diantha Dorchester?"

"Yes, but my friends call me Didi."

The chief inspector looked at her, his eyebrows scrunched up, glowering.

"Um, but you are not my friend, so Diantha is fine." She looked at her sister and shrugged, suppressing a giggle.

The chief inspector asked her some more standard questions and then inquired about her whereabouts during the game.

"No, I did not go back to the house," she said, her lovely eyes wide. "I did sit down once or twice to have some lemonade, though. It was a very relaxed activity with lots of time between turns."

"And was you sister present the entire time?" His brows were knitted. Didi looked at her sister. "Yes," she replied. "She and Julian, Mr. Jeffries, were together for the whole game."

The chief inspector quirked an eyebrow. "Did you notice anyone leave the party and go to the house?" he continued.

"Actually, my partner, Marcus popped back to the house to use the facilities, but he was only gone for ten minutes or so. We didn't even have to miss our turn."

The ubiquitous book received the facts.

"Did you notice anything else that might be pertinent, Miss Dorchester?"

Didi placed her fist under her chin and looked heavenward, presenting a very pretty picture.

"I don't think so," she said.

"Thank you for your time, Miss Dorchester," said the chief inspector. Inspector Hornby stood and opened the door for her. As she exited, Didi caught her sister's eye, tilted her head towards the chief inspector and raised her eyebrows.

Next on the agenda was Octavia Farrington. As she came through the door, she appeared to have aged ten years. Her mouth sagged at the corners and she seemed bone weary. She glanced at Dodo and gave a half-hearted smile that did not reach her eyes.

"Please, sit down Mrs. Farrington. I appreciate that this must be a stressful time for you, so I will try to make this as quick as possible." Octavia vaguely nodded and brought a hankie to her nose.

"Did you participate in the game of croquet?"

"Yes, I was partnered with my son, Freddy." She sighed, bending her head and pushing her hands through her hair. Dodo noticed that her hands shook slightly,

"Were you present for the entire game?"

"Yes."

"And what about your son?"

The lines on her face deepened. "I believe so. I was much worried about the Alexanders you know, and I was trying to keep up a pretense of brightness because the theft had put such a damper on things. I kept jollying everyone along, though I really just wanted to sneak back to the house and curl up in bed until the whole nastiness had been dealt with."

And have a drink…

"Understandable," said the chief inspector "Did you notice anyone go back to the house during play?" His tone was casual, but leaning forward, Dodo noticed a new intensity burning in his eyes.

Octavia closed her eyes, lifting her chin and breathing deeply, then a slight frown creased her brow and she opened her eyes to look directly at Dodo as though she had realized something. She swiftly wiped the frown away and looked straight at the chief inspector. "No, I don't believe I did."

Dodo shifted uncomfortably in her seat. She was sure Octavia had just lied to the chief inspector. But why?

"How long have you known the Alexanders?"

The change in topics evidently caught Octavia by surprise as she blinked rapidly, but she quickly recovered. "We've known the Colonel since the ark, that was when he was married to his first wife. We've known Anne since before they were married. I set them up you know."

"Are they financially secure?"

A splash of color mottled Octavia's cheeks. "I'm sure I don't know, Chief Inspector! It's not the kind of thing we ask each other at dinner parties you know." She was clearly scandalized.

Undeterred by his apparent faux pas, the chief inspector pushed on. "I understand that, Mrs. Farrington, but sometimes we learn these things through the grapevine."

"I don't approve of gossip," she declared piously.

Score one for Octavia!

The chief inspector paused. "Your husband did not participate in the game, I understand. Do you know where he was?"

Octavia's eyes came alive for the first time since entering the room. "What are you insinuating, Chief Inspector?" She lifted her spine, head high.

"Nothing," he said, gently. "It is a standard question, Mrs. Farrington. Knowing where he was may help us rule him out as a suspect."

Octavia slumped again, beaten. "He had gone to get one of his golf clubs fixed. It had troubled him during the golf outing the day before."

"Thank you." He shuffled some papers on the desk. "That will be all for now, unless anyone else has a question?"

Dodo seized the opportunity. "How long had Agnes been working here?"

"About three years. She came to us straight from school. She began as a parlor maid and was then trained up as a lady's maid when my old maid retired," Octavia replied.

"Was her work satisfactory?"

"Adequate, I would describe it. It is so terribly hard to find good staff these days and we put up with a great deal that we never would have before the Great War. Agnes was a little too chatty at times and prone to be late coming back from her afternoon off, but generally she was suitable."

"Did she get along with the other staff?" continued Dodo.

"On the whole, though I think she gave herself airs. She was quite young for a lady's maid and that didn't always sit well downstairs."

There was another pause. The chief inspector looked at Inspector Hornby who shook his head and Octavia was dismissed.

"What did you pick up from her?" asked the chief inspector of Dodo.

Dodo decided not to share her impression that Octavia had not told the whole truth, preferring to question her alone. She said instead, "I think we are building a picture of Agnes that is less than flattering. I have a theory that Agnes knew who the thief was and decided to blackmail them – this would explain the stockings and the talk of coming into money. If I am right, and Agnes had told Octavia that she knew who the thief was right away, instead of blackmailing them, I believe she would be alive today."

Chapter 12

Anne Alexander colored, unexpectedly. "Insured? Of course, my jewels were insured, but they are irreplaceable, Chief Inspector."

"I understand that you are quite the collector. That must become very expensive."

Dodo saw Anne glance at her and then at the floor. "Yes, it is rather."

"But you have the necessary means?"

There was a beat before Anne replied, "Of course." The color on her cheek betrayed her.

"And how much were the jewels insured for?"

"Three hundred thousand pounds." Her face was strangely rigid.

The chief inspector failed to hide his surprise and let out a low whistle. "Was that the value of the necklace?" he croaked.

Anne let her fingers slide over the modest pearls she was wearing before answering quietly. "No."

"I beg your pardon?" the chief inspector said.

"No. The jewels were worth one hundred thousand pounds."

Chief inspector Blood leaned back in his chair making it creak in protest. "Are you in the habit of insuring your jewels for that much more than they are worth?" he asked, incredulously.

"Yes," she said with a hint of defiance. "It is not unusual, I can assure you. Pieces such as this, with this type of provenance, go up in value all the time."

"Then what is making you so uncomfortable, if I may ask?"

Anne Alexander straightened her skirt before answering. "Well, it's just, in this instance it might appear that, well that, we had a motive to lose them."

"Do you?" asked the chief inspector, pitching forward.

"No! Certainly not!" Blotches splashed onto her neck.

Methinks the lady doth protest too much.

The chief inspector let a few moments pass, allowing Anne's defiance to settle into the room before asking, "The maid, Agnes. Had you met her before?"

"We are frequent visitors here, chief inspector. Yes, I had met the maid before." Anne clasped her hands tightly around her crossed legs.

"Had she waited on you in the past?"

"A couple of times. Sometimes when we travel, I give my maid the time off as her mother is in bad health." She pressed her pearls against her neck.

"Was Agnes satisfactory as a lady's maid?"

"I knew that she was being trained by Tavie - Mrs. Farrington, and so I made certain concessions. There was plenty of room for improvement, but the girl is young-" Anne's face paled— "oh, I mean, she was young."

"May I ask a question?" asked Dodo, scooting forward in her chair.

The chief inspector growled as Dodo deliberately and wantonly broke his ground rules but nodded his head.

"Did you find Agnes to be honest?" continued Dodo.

Anne pursed her lips, considering the question, obviously relieved to have moved on from the matter of insurance. "I think she was a snoop, interested in sparkly things, but I've never had anything go missing before. She was no thief, but I wouldn't put it past her to try on my things when I was not there."

"Is that why you did not allow her access to your portable safe?" Dodo asked.

"Yes. I would trust my own maid with my life but not someone else's maid. She had no loyalty to me, and I thought it prudent not to lead her into temptation."

"And yet you did not put the necklace away that night?" interrupted Inspector Hornby.

"No. It was most unusual for me, but I was frightfully tired and had drunk one too many glasses of wine. I just thought I'd put it away in the morning but then we overslept and had to hurry for the golf outing, and I forgot. I regret it now of course, but one does not expect to be robbed at one's friend's house."

"No, indeed," agreed Dodo.

"You think the two crimes are connected then?" asked Anne with genuine surprise.

Chief Inspector Blood jumped back in, clearly annoyed that Dodo had hi-jacked the interview and unwilling to cede her more territory. "We are not far enough into the investigation to form any opinion on that, Mrs. Alexander," he said. "Did you or your husband return to the house at any time during the croquet game?"

"No," she replied.

"You are certain that neither of you needed the facilities," Chief Inspector Blood pursued.

Again, a pause. "No, we were getting ready to head in for that purpose when we heard the scream."

He nodded. "Hornby. Any more questions for Mrs. Alexander?"

"No but be assured that I have men looking for the necklace," Hornby said to Anne. "I am still the lead detective on that case and am pursuing every lead."

"Thank you, Inspector."

"Anything else?" said the chief inspector, eyeing Dodo.

She shook her head though she was eager to find out why the question of insurance had caused the lady to shrink. Perhaps she would make some calls later.

"Thank you, Mrs. Alexander. We may need to talk to you again."

"Of course," she said, rising to leave.

When the door was securely closed, the chief inspector turned to Inspector Hornby and said, "I need you to contact their bank and check that their finances are as robust as she claims. I have the nagging feeling she was holding out on us."

"Yes, sir," replied Inspector Hornby and left the room as Mr. Alexander entered.

Arthur Alexander's face was flushed, and Dodo noticed a sheen of sweat on his upper lip. *Curious.*

"Please take a seat," said the chief inspector, motioning toward the chair.

"Your wife has explained that the missing necklace was insured for three times its value."

Straight for the throat!

Arthur blinked before responding, hesitantly. "Yes. Is that a crime?"

"Not at all. But it does tell me that, apart from the intrinsic value of such a piece, the theft would not cause you financial distress. Quite the opposite in fact."

If it were possible, Arthur Alexander's face turned more crimson. "Look here, if you are suggesting that I stole the jewels myself to defraud the insurance company, I vigorously object to the insinuation, sir!"

The chief inspector took no action to diffuse the offense and instead said, "I am not. I am merely pointing out that if you had concocted such a plan with your wife, you would have done so in the privacy of your room, putting the jewels in a secure place that even a nosy maid would not find. No one would have been any the wiser. In such an event, you would have no reason to kill the maid as she would not have witnessed the deception."

An array of expressions passed over the Colonel's face as he tried to decide if the chief inspector was accusing him of anything. Instead he grunted like a disgruntled bulldog.

"However, my concern at the present is with the murder. I cannot suppose that one crime had anything to do with the other, therefore I must ask, did you leave the croquet game at any time before the discovery of the murdered maid?"

Dodo could not help noticing that the chief inspector was a lot less delicate with the Colonel than he had been with the ladies.

The Colonel stroked his moustache as he thought back. "No. We were about to go back to the house when the hue and cry went up," he said.

"Thank you, you are free to go."

"Uh," interrupted Dodo eliciting a grimace and a scowl from the chief inspector. She pushed on. "May I ask the provenance of the necklace?"

Colonel Alexander sat back in his chair and made a tent of his fingers. "Legend has it that the necklace belonged to the Queen of Sheba who presented it to King Solomon. There is, however, no concrete evidence of that. We do have records indicating that it belonged to a Chinese Empress in the 12th Century, and that it was handed down to her posterity. We bought it from a descendant in need of funds."

"How fascinating," replied Dodo.

"If that's all…," said the Colonel pushing himself to his feet.

"Yes, thank you Colonel."

"Chief Inspector," began Dodo after the Colonel was safely out of the room, "I can confirm that my father insures his valuables for more than they are worth. It is not unusual among the upper classes. And the provenance! A piece with that kind of history could easily see a large spike in value."

The chief inspector's face hardened. "I am not a complete ignoramus, Lady Dorothea! I am fully aware of the vagaries of the market for antique jewelry. Furthermore, you interrupted when I clearly stated that you should only speak when invited!" The tip of his nose had turned a cherry red.

"But you *didn't* invite me," she purred, "and I thought the provenance might be important. If the two cases are linked…"

"We cannot assume that with no evidence," he replied, shuffling his papers around.

"Aren't you a teeny bit interested by the jewels' history?" she persisted.

"Not really," he growled. "Now, who's next?"

A gentle tap at the door heralded the arrival of Anita Anderson. The chief inspector asked her all the usual questions. She stated that she had not gone back to the house but thought that her partner for the game, Charlie, might have. "I wasn't really paying attention. When it wasn't our turn we were sitting and drinking and chatting, Chief Inspector. It was a very casual affair and more than once we had to cajole the players to get back to the game."

The chief inspector examined his notebook and made a great show of looking something up. Dodo was intrigued. *What was he up to?*

"You live next door, I understand."

"Yes."

"You have known the family your whole life, then?"

"Yes."

"Are you romantically involved with Freddy Farrington?"

Anita started with surprise and then broke into a belly laugh. "Haha! Oh no, Chief Inspector! Haha! What a funny idea! Haha! Freddy is not my type at all. We have been friends since we were young but that is all. Haha!"

Dodo had the good grace to feel sorry for poor Freddy and was glad he was not here to witness the scene. It took Anita a few moments to regain her composure. The chief inspector watched Anita carefully.

Finally, he spoke. "Do you have an appointment to keep, Miss Anderson? Several guests have noticed you looking at your watch a great deal?"

That had been a dart to the heart.

Anita immediately sobered, red blossoming on her peachy cheeks.

"What an odd question, Chief Inspector," she began slowly. "I don't see how that has anything to do with the current situation but since you ask, no. I got this watch as a gift recently and I am getting used to wearing it." The response rang hollow, but the chief did not question her on it further.

"You knew the maid, Agnes, I suppose. What did you think of her?"

"Chief Inspector, she was a servant. I had no dealings with her at all." Dodo caught a slight wince from the chief inspector at the response, but he recovered quickly.

"Is there anything else that you know that might have a bearing on the case?" he continued.

"It is a terribly unfortunate thing, but I have no information that I believe would help you," Anita said in a clipped staccato. "Though I would love to be able to deflect suspicion from myself."

"That is all, thank you," said the chief inspector

What? He wasn't going to ask her about the jewels? Dodo jumped in before Anita had a chance to escape. "What did you think of Mrs. Alexander's emeralds?"

If looks could kill, the chief inspector would be charged with murder himself. She ignored the glare and the grunting.

"I thought they were rather gaudy if you must know," Anita replied. "My taste runs to the more delicate," she added as she fingered the dainty gold chain around her neck.

Well, that was most certainly a lie. There was nothing gaudy about them. Why was she so eager to appear indifferent?

"Are you quite finished Lady Dorothea?" demanded the chief inspector, clearly struggling to keep his voice level.

Dodo arranged her features into the most innocent expression possible and pronounced, "Yes. Yes, thank you Anita."

The chief inspector allowed Anita to leave and was about to lay into Dodo when Inspector Hornby returned.

Saved.

"I used the telephone to call the Yard about the Alexander's finances, sir, and while they were at it, I asked them to look into everyone's. They'll get a warrant of course."

The chief inspector exhaled, still glowering at Dodo. "Good initiative Hornby. My instincts tell me that a lack of money is at the root of both cases."

"You are assuming that the two cases are related then?" said Dodo.

"I'm not a big believer in coincidences, Lady Dorothea. Do you have another idea?"

"I tend to agree but I've been thinking, should we not also consider the possibility that they are *not* connected? Obviously, the theft would have to be about money, but what if, say, the murder was committed to protect someone from suspicion of the theft? Or, Agnes was murdered because she is a nasty piece of work and upset someone unconnected with the jewel theft?"

The chief inspector scratched his chin, clearly wrestling with the idea of giving any credit to her ideas. He finally said, "Those are possibilities, yes, but at this point and from my experience, I am pretty sure one person committed both crimes. Two crimes in one location around the same time frame…the second was likely an attempt to cover up the first."

Dodo remained diplomatically silent and smoothed her dress as Chief Inspector Blood made more notes.

Marcus shuffled in and slouched in his chair, arms folded, oozing disdain. Even now, he couldn't manage some respect for the other people in the room.

"Your name is Marcus Makepeace, I understand."

"Well done!" said Marcus in a tone dripping with sarcasm.

Dodo shot him a warning look to which Marcus merely shrugged.

The chief inspector's pupils narrowed, and his nostrils flared dangerously. Marcus was walking on thin ice if she was not mistaken. The chief inspector then grabbed his pencil roughly and scrunched his nose as though a terrible smell had invaded the room. Dodo noted a new fire in his eyes.

After a second, he said with icy coldness, "How do you know the Farringtons?"

"I've known them for years. Freddy and I were at Eton together and they often invited me to stay and vice versa." He sounded like an insufferable snob.

"Did you go back to the house during the croquet game?"

Marcus made a pantomime of considering the question and eventually said, "No, I don't think so?"

"Are you absolutely sure," asked the chief inspector.

Dodo held her breath as he sprung the trap.

"Yes!" declared Marcus.

"What would you say if I told you that a witness has already told me that you returned to the house to use the facilities?"

The first signs of discomfort suffused Marcus' face and he sat up. "Um, then perhaps I did. I really don't remember." His insolent tone was draining away.

"Mr. Makepeace, a young woman has been murdered by someone in the house. It is in your best interests to be completely honest with me. You were seen entering the house." The chief inspector let the statement hang between them.

"I say, you're not suggesting that it was me, are you? This is exactly why I didn't tell you that I went inside. I had nothing to do with that girl's death, I tell you!"

The chief inspector pounced. "Really?"

"Of course not! I didn't even know the silly girl!" Marcus' face was clouding with concern and he sat up straight.

"You just said that you are a frequent guest in this house. You must have known her."

"I've seen her of course, but she was a servant. I didn't speak to her. She was background." The pinched look returned to the chief inspector's face.

"She was a person, Mr. Makepeace."

"Yes, yes, of course. I didn't mean anything by it."

"So, you did know her, and she would have known you, and you came back to the house around the time of the murder."

"I say, you're twisting my words. Why would I have need to murder a lady's maid?" His voice was rising in pitch, and Dodo sensed that he was beginning to panic.

"That is the question, isn't it, sir? Who had a motive to kill this young woman? We have reason to believe that the murder may be connected to the theft. I am sure you would have known the value of the emerald necklace brought here by Mrs. Alexander. Perhaps you were in need of money?"

Dodo detected a strange expression pass fleetingly over Marcus' face. *Surely not?*

"Of course not!" he protested, but with less enthusiasm than the situation warranted.

Chief Inspector Blood remained silent, appearing to wait for the discomfort of quietness to work its magic.

Marcus flashed a look at Dodo as though he was pleading with her to throw him a lifeline. She merely stared back. He had not endeared himself to her this weekend. He shifted frantic eyes, maneuvering in his seat, gripping the sides of the chair. "Why would I need money? I'm the only son of one of the finest families in England," he said, his voice was trailing off.

"Well, we shall see," replied the chief inspector, ominously.

Dodo had the distinct impression that he was enjoying this worm on the line.

"Now that we have established that you did in fact return to the house, what did you see?" he asked, "I believe all the bathrooms are on the upper floor?" This last was directed to Dodo. She nodded.

Marcus took a deep breath. "I saw no one. The house was unusually quiet."

"Did you see Agnes Brown while you were upstairs?"

This time the answer was given with much more confidence. "No. No I am sure I did not. No one was upstairs when I went up. I came out of my bathroom and ran back down the stairs so that I would not hold up the game." The only response was the scratching of the chief inspector's pencil. Marcus rubbed his neck, watching.

"What time was this?"

"I can't be sure, but I would say it was around three."

"Hornby, any questions?"

The inspector shook his head.

"Lady Dorothea?" He strung the words out.

"Just a tiny one. Did you notice if the door to the Alexander's room was open or closed?"

"I don't know. Closed I think."

"Right, that will be all for now," said the chief inspector.

Marcus practically fled the room.

"You enjoyed that, didn't you sir?" said Inspector Hornby with a grin.

Chief Inspector Blood rubbed his chin. "Yes, yes I did! Smarmy kid!"

Dodo wanted to take umbridge on behalf of her class, but in this instance, she was in total agreement with the chief inspector.

Chapter 13

Charlie, athletic and tanned, appeared uncharacteristically ill at ease, fingering his collar and pulling his jacket close around him. Dodo had never seen him this way. In fact, he was the kind of person one might envy as always being confident and in control. Did he have something to hide?

The chief inspector was guiding him through the general questions he had asked everyone, and Charlie was answering in a flat, monotone.

"Did you come back to the house during the game? I believe Miss Anderson was your partner." Charlie's eyes darted around the room several times and then he seemed to get a grip on himself. "No, I don't think I did."

"You don't think so?" said the chief inspector with a hint of accusation in his tone. Charlie slid back in his seat. "I mean, I did not."

"Did your partner, Miss Anderson, come back to the house at any time during the game?" Charlie stroked his chin with his hand, thinking. "No," he finally said.

"Are you sure?"

"Yes, yes, completely sure. We had lots of lemonade as it was thirsty work but neither of us left the game. I'm quite certain."

"Do you know anything about the theft of the emeralds?"

Charlie looked as shocked as if the chief inspector had slapped him. The change of subject was so sudden. "No, of course not. I know nothing about jewels. They could have been paste for all I know." The chief inspector looked up quickly as if struck by something and then scribbled in the notebook.

"And you did not know the maid, Agnes Brown?"

"No. I visited this house a few times when I was at Eton, but Agnes was not here then. Before this weekend I had never met her."

"Did you 'meet' her this time?"

"Chief Inspector!" blurted out Dodo aghast.

"That is not what I meant," said Charlie, smiling weakly at Dodo. "To be honest, I hadn't even noticed her and couldn't describe her now if you asked me to." This was said with more energy than anything else he had yet said, and Dodo was sure he was being honest.

"Did you know the emeralds would be here this weekend?"

"I have never met the Alexanders before and did not know they were coming. So, no. I did not."

"Thank you, Mr. Chadwick. I will probably need to question you again but that is all for now."

While Chief Inspector Blood wrote, Charlie caught Dodo's eye and dragged a finger across his throat. She smiled with sympathy as he headed for the door.

The chief inspector swung forcibly towards Dodo once Charlie was gone. "I have warned you about interrupting me!" he cried. "One more outburst like that and you will be gone!"

"Well, I found that question most inappropriate," she declared, holding her ground.

"An interrogation does not concern itself with what is deemed appropriate, Lady Dorothea. We are seeking the truth."

He was right, but she hated to see her friends painted into corners.

"Of course," she said by way of apology.

After a minute, the chief inspector continued. "How well do you know him?"

Dodo tilted her silky head down and regarded the chief inspector through her long, black lashes. "Ages. He's a lovely chap. Wouldn't hurt a fly."

"He seemed…shifty," Chief Inspector Blood responded. "Don't you agree Hornby?"

The inspector nodded. "Much too attractive for his own good that one."

"Not a bit of it!" said Dodo, leaping once more to Charlie's defense. "He was nervous of you to be sure, but not because he has anything to hide, I'd swear to it!"

"Have you been romantically involved with Mr. Chadwick?"

"No!" said Dodo with enthusiasm. "No, nothing like that. We are just very good friends and he is so…nice."

"N.i.c.e," said the chief inspector as he wrote the word in his book.

Dodo scowled. She was about to make a stinging comment when the door opened again and in came Julian, and all her indignation blew away.

Julian glanced at her with a nervous smile and then looked deliberately at the chief inspector. His broad shoulders were tense, and his chin had a determined look about it. There was no hint of flirtation with her today.

After the initial questions had been asked, the chief inspector plunged the knife right in. "Did you kill Agnes Brown?"

Dodo's brows rose in shock. Why he chose to interrogate some suspects so directly, she had no idea. It was hardly subtle.

Dodo was perplexed to see that Julian's stiffness dissolved under the weight of the question, and he appeared to relax in the chair. "No, of course not." There was no suggestion of defensiveness in his tone, nor in his posture.

The chief inspector regarded him thoughtfully for a moment and then seemed to come to a decision of some sort. "Mr. Jeffries, have you seen anything unusual this weekend that might have something to do with either the theft or the murder?"

Now the expression on Julian's face altered, and he appeared to be deliberating. Dodo shifted forward in her chair. "I hope this isn't gossiping, Chief Inspector," he began, "and I am sure it has nothing to do with either crime…"

"Anything of interest may have a bearing on the case. Let me be the judge," said the chief inspector, sitting up, pencil poised.

"Well, I was up very late last night trying to get some milk from the kitchen when I heard something and peeked out to see Anita slipping through the side door that is kept unlocked. She was returning from somewhere outside, and it was apparent that she did not know that anyone had seen her. She walked quietly along the corridor and up the stairs to her room. In and of itself, it is not particularly suspicious, but given the circumstances and the lateness of the hour…" He let his words hang in the air.

The two policemen exchanged looks. Dodo's eyes moved to Julian who had an apology written on his face.

"Have you asked her about it?" continued the chief inspector.

"I tried to make a joke that hinted at it, and she told me that she had no idea to what I was referring. Rather odd, that."

"She only lives next door. She could have run home for something," said Dodo. The chief inspector glared at her, and she was mature enough to admit that she had broken his rules again and offered a sheepish smile in apology. She put a finger to her lips.

"Indeed," said the chief inspector. "Is there anything else?"

Dodo noticed a slight tightening of the shoulders again, but Julian merely replied, "No."

The chief inspector excused him.

"Well, well, well," sang Chief Inspector Blood. "I don't buy your notion about running home at that hour. I wonder what Miss Anderson was up to so late at night and alone. She failed to share *that* information with us!"

"It could be something else perfectly innocent," Dodo defended, more because of her dislike of the chief inspector than because she believed it.

"In a murder investigation, it is my experience that no unusual behavior is 'perfectly innocent' Miss Dorchester. Hornby, let's set a tail on her and see if she goes out tonight. I'd like to know more about her nocturnal activities." He turned sharply and directed his next comment to Dodo. "And you had better not warn her about the tail or you will be excluded from any further police business, whatever Sir Matthew Cusworth might have to say about it!"

Dodo lifted her hand in a sharp salute and declared, "You have my word, Chief Inspector."

Inspector Hornby stifled a grin.

Freddy poked his head around the door.

"Come in!" said Blood.

As he walked by, Dodo sniffed. *Was that whiskey?*

"How well did you know Agnes Brown?" barked the chief inspector.

Freddy lifted his brows high in surprise. "She is—was—my mother's maid. I hardly knew her at all." He cut his eyes over to Dodo in search of an advocate. She shrugged to let him know she was surprised at the chief inspector's tone but held her tongue. She had to admit, she had a soft spot for Freddy.

"But you must have seen her about the house," the chief inspector pursued.

"I suppose so. I don't pay much attention to the staff."

Chief Inspector Blood chewed his pencil. "Did you return to the house during the game of croquet?"

"Now there, I know I did not. Not at any time, though I did run back to the house when the alarm went up."

"Yes, you were the first person to see the body. How did you come upon her?"

"I heard the screaming coming from the house and ran straight to see what was amiss. I found Maisie, hands to her face, screaming the place down. She was standing over Agnes who was sprawled on the floor."

"What did you do then?"

"I grabbed Maisie and shook her out of her hysteria and took her down to the kitchen for Mrs. McCreedy to deal with. Then I told the housekeeper to call the police and ran outside to tell everyone what had happened."

"Did you touch anything? The body? The scarf?"

"No. I know enough not to do that, Chief Inspector."

"You didn't check to see if Agnes was alive?"

"It was pretty obvious that she was not. I was in shock. I had never seen a dead body and just wanted to get away. I did not go back upstairs. I needed to get back to people."

The chief inspector took some time writing this down before asking the next question.

Freddy rolled his neck and shoulders.

"Mrs. Alexander's jewels. Do you know what they are worth?"

Freddy frowned. "I don't know exactly, only that Mother was thrilled she was bringing them because of their provenance. So, I would guess they are worth a packet!" He tried to smile at his little joke but failed.

The chief inspector coughed. "Do you know anything about their theft?"

"Me? Goodness, no! Why would I know anything?" He looked to Dodo.

"Perhaps you saw or heard something?" the chief inspector continued.

"Not me, I can assure you. The first I heard of it was at breakfast. Terrible thing. Mother is distraught. Totally. It was supposed to have been a lovely weekend and it has turned out really awful. Poor mother, I don't think she can stand much more."

"I understand you visited the dentist before the croquet?" The pencil was pointed at Freddy.

"Ah, yes…is that a crime now?" He tried laughing again but sounded like a strangled cat.

"May I ask what the problem was?"

"I, uh, chipped my tooth last week and thought I would get it seen to after the weekend, but it became very painful, so I got seen on an emergency basis."

"Your neighbor, Miss Anderson. Have you ever been romantically involved?"

"With Anita? No, but not for want of trying!" He rocked back in his chair and slapped his thigh.

The chief inspector's face remained like stone, and Freddy ran a nervous hand through his hair. "She has refused my advances on many occasions. I've given up. But she is good company, for the most part. Mother invited her."

"Well, I think that's it," Chief Inspector Blood said, "unless you have any other information that you think might be relevant?"

Freddy sucked in his cheeks, all trace of humor gone and looked at the chief inspector with his chin dipped. "I feel terribly disloyal but…" He paused.

The chief inspector leaned forward. "In a murder investigation, loyalties must be put aside," he assured in a quiet, firm tone.

"Oh, this isn't about the murder!" Freddy said with horror. "I just was thinking about who might be in need of money and I happen to know that Charlie has a bit of a gambling problem. He told me. He recently suffered some serious losses."

Dodo opened her mouth in shock, but no words came out. *Charlie a gambler?*

"Is that so?" responded the chief inspector with a glint in his eye. "That is very useful information. We will be sure to follow up on that, young Mr. Farrington."

"You won't have to tell him that *I* told you, will you?" said Freddy with a pained expression.

"I don't see why that would be necessary, sir," said Chief inspector Blood.

Freddy stood and waited until the chief inspector showed him the door.

"Well!" exploded Dodo. "I never would have thought. I've been friends with Charlie for years. We tend to run in the same circles, and that's the first I've ever heard of it!"

"In my experience," began the chief inspector, "people are very clever at hiding their vices. I once arrested a man who had been smuggling children in an illegal adoption scheme. His wife had no idea. He had three children of his own and they all lived in an upper middleclass neighborhood. He told her he was in insurance."

"Incredible!" gasped Dodo.

"If people put the same intelligence and hard work into legitimate schemes as they do their criminal ones, they could earn a lucrative, honest living," continued the chief inspector. "One chap was running a—"

A knock on the door interrupted them. "Ah, Mr. Farrington, do come in," continued the chief inspector.

Mr. Richard Farrington had the same downtrodden look that his wife had exhibited. Dodo suspected that they would not be having any parties for some time.

"Now," said the chief inspector gently, "I am sorry that this has to be done, but justice must be served."

"Of course, of course," blustered Mr. Farrington. "Ask away." There was no enthusiasm in the command and Dodo suddenly felt very sorry for him.

"I understand that you were away from the house during the croquet. Is that correct?"

"Yes, my best putter got bent during the golf outing, and I went into town to get it fixed."

"What time did you leave?"

"Around noon," Mr. Farrington replied.

"I suppose the golf shop can verify that?"

"Oh, yes. Yes, they keep very good records."

"And what time did you return?"

"I stayed, as Phil, the owner of the golf shop, said they could see to it immediately. I spend rather a lot of money there, Chief Inspector, and whenever I need something, they jump right to it."

"I bet they do!" said the chief inspector with a wry grin.

"I got back about four o' clock to a great hubbub of activity and emotions. My poor wife was done in, I can tell you. And the poor girl—"

"Yes," interrupted the chief inspector. "Four hours. That is a long time to wait."

"Oh, I popped into the pub, The Dog and Whistle. Bert the bar man will vouch for that. We had a long conversation about the state of golf in this country."

"Very good. And the missing jewels…"

"That is dashed embarrassing. One does not expect to have one's guests stolen from," said Mr. Farrington with more energy. "I am quite at a loss—unless you think that Agnes stole them?"

"No, sir. We have no reason to think that. In fact, we believe that she may have witnessed the theft and been murdered by the thief to keep her quiet."

"Oh, my!" exclaimed Mr. Farrington, rubbing his hand down his face. "I feel that I am in some awful nightmare and keep hoping to wake up!"

"I understand, sir. Do you have any information about the jewel theft that might be helpful?"

"I know that Anne feels terribly guilty for not putting the jewels in her safe. If she had, there would have been no opportunity for the thief and then no murder!"

"Lady Dorothea, do you have any questions?"

Caught off guard for a moment that he had invited her, she jumped at the chance. There was a question she had been itching to ask all weekend. "Are you and Tavie under any duress that began before the party?" she asked.

Mr. Farrington blushed brightly and looked daggers at Dodo as though he wished she would vanish. "What the…" he blustered and then seemed to remember his manners. "No, of course not. Everything is fine."

Dodo remained unconvinced.

Chapter 14

All the suspects had now been interviewed and the two inspectors huddled to discuss their findings. Not being invited to the party, Dodo got up to leave which caught the chief inspector's attention.

"I hope you will report anything of interest that comes to light with your friends?" he said.

"As you so rightly pointed out, Chief Inspector, there cannot be any loyalties when investigating a murder, even when it involves one's friends."

"Would you be open to doing a little unofficial snooping?" he continued. Dodo cocked her head. Perhaps she was moving from enemy to ally.

"If it can bring justice for that young girl, I would be happy to snoop," she responded.

"Just a couple more things, Lady Dorothea," continued the chief inspector. "Please let everyone know that I am giving them permission to leave the house and go as far as the village until this evening."

Dodo brightened.

"And, this person has murdered once, and possibly to protect themselves. In my experience, such a person would not hesitate to murder again. Watch your back, Lady Dorothea."

"If I didn't know better, I would think you were worried about me Chief Inspector Blood!" And she left the room in a swirl of organza.

***

Once in her room Dodo set about writing down the things she could remember from the interviews and then made a list of questions.

1. What was Anita up to?

She did not know Anita very well. Although she lived next door to Farrington Hall, Anita had not come over very much when the Dorchesters had visited in the past. The few times Dodo did remember meeting her she had seemed like a spoiled child who pouted when she did not get her own way in a game. But how many of us would fare well if we were judged as adults by our behavior as children?

During this weekend Anita had been pleasant enough, though definitely distracted. Could it have something to do with the crimes? She was not someone Dodo would naturally gravitate to as a particular friend, but maybe it was time to make an effort in order to discover more about her.

2. *Was Charlie a gambler?*

Freddy had said so. As much as Dodo could not believe it, she supposed it would be easy enough to check into. She had developed some shady contacts when investigating the horse problem for her father. She could leverage those.

3. *What were the Alexanders hiding?*

Were they really having financial problems as the chief inspector had suggested? He had set the ball rolling to look into that and she would wait to see what that materialized.

4. *Why did Marcus initially lie about going back to the house?*

So far, he was the only person who had been forced to admit to returning. She supposed that made him the prime suspect at this point. Much as she disliked him, she did not really believe him capable of murder, or clever enough for theft.

5. *What was wrong with Octavia?*

Dodo was sure Octavia had remembered something that made her uncomfortable during her interview that she did not want to tell the chief inspector. Perhaps Dodo could coax it out of her. And why was Octavia drinking so heavily? It obviously pre-dated the current unpleasantness. And drunkenness was so unattractive.

6. *Freddy. Why was* he *drinking and why was the chief inspector so interested in his tooth ache?*

She hoped Freddy wasn't succumbing to the lure of alcohol like his mother. She could take the initiative and pay a visit to the Farrington's dentist she supposed, but at this point she did not see how it related to anything.

7. *Why did Julian go pale at the mention of car crashes?*

Her curiosity had certainly been piqued. She would have to put her personal feelings aside and be objective. Was he hiding a secret he was willing to commit murder to hide? A quick trip to the library might be in order.

She hid the list under her pillow and went in search of Didi whom she found playing billiards with Charlie and Julian.

"The chief inspector has said we can go as far as the village, so I'm just going to pop out for a bit," Dodo explained.

"Hurrah for that!" whooped Didi. "Perhaps we can get some dinner at the pub later and give poor Octavia a break."

The suggestion garnered murmurs of approval.

As she was leaving Farrington Hall, Dodo saw Anita up ahead and ran to catch up. "I'm going to the village. You?" she asked.

"The chief inspector said I could go home since it's right next door, and he has done his initial interviews. I can't leave altogether but at least I can go for a bit. It's so…strained, don't you think? Everyone looking sideways at one another."

"Yes. The murder has spooked everyone," said Dodo.

"And it has to be one of us really, doesn't it?" continued Anita with a slight shiver.

They had reached the end of the long driveway and Anita peeled off to the left toward her home. Dodo toyed with the idea of following her to see if she was really going home, but it was full light and there were no places to hide. It would be very awkward if she tried playing detective and got caught. Best to leave that to the constables.

The walk to the village was two miles of pretty country lanes dotted with black and white, wattle and daub Elizabethan cottages amid soft meadows. The village itself was traditional with a pond, a village green and one pub. It also had a small library as she had hoped it would. She quickly popped in making sure no one saw her and went up to the librarian, a middle-aged woman with a steel gray, tight bun and pince-nez. She was so stereotypical Dodo had to hide a grin behind her hand.

"Good afternoon," Dodo began. The woman looked up, eyes narrowed, as though she was irritated to be disturbed but Dodo pressed on. "I say, I know you are a very small library..."

The librarian's expression pinched even further as she bristled with offense at the perceived slight.

"Oh, I am sure that you have everything necessary," Dodo continued quickly. "I am hoping that you can help me find some back issues of a local paper for Sudbury in Essex?"

"We don't stock such things here, of course," said the middle-aged woman, "but I can make a telephone call to the main library of Suffolk and have a research assistant look it up for us and call me back. Will that suffice?"

"That would be absolutely marvelous!" gushed Dodo, cranking up her patented smile.

"What are the dates you are interested in?"

Dodo gave her the details and told the librarian she would come back.

Before heading back to Farrington Hall, she spotted a bright red telephone box and placed a call to an old friend who knew Marcus.

After a long conversation, she managed to bring round the topic around to Marcus, and learned some potentially incriminating things, noting them in a little book. She would have to share these facts with the chief inspector.

After one more call to a bookie in Southwark, she soberly left the booth. People did get themselves in a pickle.

***

All the young people, except Anita, had decided to go to the pub for dinner both to give the Farrington's a break and to shake off the mood that pervaded the house.

Though they chatted and laughed as they walked like any other group of young adults, it was more than a little forced. However, when they entered the pub, the cloak of suspicion and fear seemed to slide off everyone. Julian sought out Dodo, but his ardor had noticeably cooled.

There was also the reality of the whopping elephant in the room, but everyone had silently agreed to ignore it for the evening.

Dodo watched everyone through the lens of the theft and the murder, however hard she tried not to. The situation was perfect for casually interviewing people while their guard was down—snooping, as the chief inspector had called it. Time to confirm some of the things she had learned this afternoon.

As everyone ate and drank, she left Julian and shifted to another position around the table, sliding in next to Charlie. She had known him for years and was sure that he'd had a crush on her at one time. There was no denying that he had improved considerably over the years, and though he was not her type, they had remained good friends. She realized that she was desperate to eliminate him as a suspect.

The babble of conversation around the table lent itself to private conversations and though talking about the murder was taboo, she felt it no deception to talk to him about his life in general. "By the way, I'm not sure I thanked you properly for helping us on the way up. You were such a savior that day," she began.

"Anyone would have done the same," he replied.

"Well, Marcus was absolutely hopeless." She grinned.

"Well, anyone but Marcus then." He laughed.

"How are things with you? I feel like we haven't had time to chat with all this ghastly business."

"Julian has pretty much taken all of your time!" he retorted.

"Yes, he has rather. Touché!" She waited.

"Well, I just finished my second year at Cambridge studying Classics. I took a year off, if you remember, hiked across the Alps. My father wants me to go into the law, but I rather fancy being a lecturer at a college. I got wanderlust during my gap year, and that would give me plenty of time to travel."

"You like the Classics enough to teach them, then?" Dodo asked. Somehow, she didn't see this athletic man as a stuffy professor.

"It's alright," he said. "But I really just want something to finance my travels, and I'm actually pretty good at it. The Classics I mean. Roger, my older brother, you remember him? He will inherit and have to take care of the estate, and I will be free as a bird but rather penniless. At least at university the students are older and a little more interested in learning. I shouldn't like to teach at a school at all!"

"Me neither!" agreed Dodo. She searched around desperately for some topic that would force him into revealing his current financial state. "I like to travel myself," she said. "I'm considering a little jaunt to Greece. Thought it might be fun to get a group together. What do you think?"

Charlie's smile slid and he made a valiant effort to pull it back. "Gosh, that sounds like a hoot, but Pops has things planned for my summer, I'm afraid." It was a weak excuse and seemed to confirm her contact's information that funds were too low for travel. Perhaps she didn't know Charlie as well as she thought she did.

"Oh, too bad?" She pouted, and noticed his eyes pinpoint her lips. She felt a little naughty about toying with his emotions, but it was a murder inquiry after all. She slid a manicured nail across the red bottom lip and watched as he breathed in deeply.

"Yes, but perhaps we could catch the band in Hyde Park one Sunday afternoon?" he said, dragging his eyes back up to hers.

She reached out and touched his arm. "That would be wonderful!"

"Then it's a date."

As long as you're not arrested for murder. The thought made her shiver and she sent it packing.

After more small talk in which she learned nothing new, she excused herself and went to the bar to get another orange juice and then shimmied her way into sitting next to Freddy. She noted that there were three empty tumblers next to his plate. *Oh, Freddy.*

"Hello, lovely!" he said, with a slight slur. Gone was the anxiety he had exhibited during the police interview, lost in the Dutch courage of the alcohol.

"Hello, Freddy," she replied, deciding to use the holiday gambit again. "I thought we might catch up a bit, you know," she continued. "What with everything, I feel like we haven't had a proper chat."

"Sure," he replied. "How are things with you?"

"Great! I'm thinking of taking a trip to Greece. Thought it might be fun to get a group to go?"

"Greece!" he purred. "Lovely islands they have. Will it be one of those?"

"I'm up for suggestions," she replied.

"I think I'd like to go," he said with a tipsy wink at her, "if I can manage to get the money from my parents. I'm a bit short these days."

Really?

"How so?" she asked with an innocent air.

He stopped and scratched his head, chewing his mouth lazily. "Well, mishandled my allowance, didn't I? Just temporary though. I'll get it sorted."

Did everyone have secret money problems?

Freddy pushed his hand through his hair and hailed the barman for another whiskey.

"When did you start drinking whiskey?" she asked with concern.

"It's great stuff. Have you tried it? Very relaxing."

"It's a bit strong for me," she replied. The barman brought another over and Freddy slurred, "Just put it on my Father's tab, Joe."

"Will do!" replied Joe.

The drunkenness made him compliant, so Dodo decided to pursue another query. "How's your tooth?"

"Tooth?"

"You know, the one you chipped. You said you went to the dentist."

His face split into a loopy grin and he tapped the side of his nose. "Fine thanks."

Though she tried to continue this line of conversation, he kept changing it to how he loathed the game of golf and she soon became bored and changed seats to sit by her sister.

***

When they returned to the house, there was a message waiting for Dodo to meet Chief Inspector Blood in the library.

"Wish me luck!" she said to Didi.

"Reporting for duty," she crowed as she entered the room.

"I was wondering if you have learned anything that might be of use to the investigation since we last spoke?"

She flashed the chief inspector a broad, pearly smile and noticed his Adam's apple drop.

"Actually, I have," she responded. "Let me see," she said as she checked her little notebook. "Ah, yes, I contacted the local librarian, who is rather a battle-axe." She dragged her mouth down to emphasize the point. "And she has contacted the library in Sudbury where a research assistant is going to look through the local papers to see if there was any kind of car accident. I simply cannot ignore how ghastly Julian looked at the mere mention of car crashes, so I thought that was worth following up."

The chief inspector who was alone, leaned back in his chair and crossed his ankles.

"I also placed a call to a mutual friend of Marcus. Would you be interested to know that he is on probation having been caught cheating on his exams at university? That might not seem particularly bad to you, Chief Inspector, but his family has a great reputation at the college and something as serious as cheating would ruin that. I think he would do anything to keep such a thing secret. He must have pleaded with them not to make it public given his family's illustrious history etc… Perhaps Agnes found out somehow and threatened to expose him? I can do some more digging. That of course, would mean that the theft and the murder were not related."

The chief inspector was punctuating her recitation with the odd, "Hmm, hmm," and "Aha." When she finished, he asked, "Is there anything else?"

"Yes, one more thing. It appears that Charlie has got himself in deep with an illegal bookie in Southwark called Boggsly." The chief inspector raised a brow. "I met a bookie on another case, and it's a tight knit community," she explained. "He happened to know all about it as it is a substantial amount of money. It appears Charlie's vice is the horses. I still cannot think of Charlie as a murderer or a thief, but this would certainly give him a motive, I'm afraid."

"It certainly does," agreed the chief inspector, sitting up in his chair.

"A quid pro quo, Chief Inspector?"

Chief Inspector Blood seemed to consider and then said, "The Alexanders are almost broke. The Colonel made a bad investment last year and it has drained their finances, so they certainly had a motive to stage the theft given that the insurance coverage was so generous. However, they would simply hide the necklace in the privacy of their own room with no witnesses, so no reason for blackmail. And Mr. Farrington was at the village pub as he claimed, giving him an alibi for the murder."

"What about Anita?" she pressed. "Has your constable found out anything?"

"Not yet, but I believe this evening may throw some light on her activities."

"And how long are you going to keep everyone here?"

"Now that we have finished the initial interviews, I think we can let everyone go home tomorrow as long as we have an address where they can be reached. Will you be staying on?"

"I think poor Tavie will be bereft if we all leave at once with this mess. Didi and I will stay a couple more days since we have nothing pressing to get back for."

"That would prove most helpful, Lady Dorothea," he said. "The divide between the classes can be problematic during an investigation of this type. Walls go up."

She blinked twice. "My goodness, Chief Inspector, that almost sounds like a compliment."

His eyes contracted. "But like I said, mind your back and don't take any unnecessary risks."

As she left the room, she blew him a cheeky kiss.

Chapter 15

"Who has a motive?" said Didi after Dodo brought her up to speed on the investigation.

"More and more people, it would seem," said Dodo, glumly. "The unintended consequence of this nasty business is that I am learning about everyone's dirty laundry! People I have known for years are showing their very human weaknesses. It puts one in an exceedingly tricky position." She took off her strappy sandals and wiggled her toes.

"So, it appears that the Alexanders and Charlie are both in dire need of funds," she continued. "That gives them the best motives, so far, for the theft. However, as the chief inspector rightly pointed out, the Alexanders could just hide the jewels in private where they would not be found by anyone else and pretend that they had been stolen to cash in on the insurance. They would have no need to murder someone, as they wouldn't have actually stolen the jewels. Charlie, on the other hand, could have stolen the necklace. He may have returned to the house during the croquet game—remember Anita wasn't sure—been seen by Agnes who threatened him, and then acted in desperation and strangled her."

"Can you really see Charlie as a murderer?" asked Didi, standing by the thick, floral curtains looking out onto the grounds.

"No, no I can't." Dodo flopped back onto the bed. "I hope it's not him – I like him too much, but I cannot ignore that he had motive, and according to Anita he may have had opportunity, and the scarf would have given him the means." She propped her head up on her elbow.

"I think we need to keep investigating to find the *real* murderer because I don't want it to be Charlie!" Didi ended, emphatically, slapping a delicate, oak occasional table and almost sending it flying.

"Marcus has disgraced his family by cheating, but I can't see a connection between him and Agnes," said Dodo.

"I much prefer him as a suspect," said Didi. "Perhaps we should look for a link?"

They both sat quietly with their thoughts for a moment.

"How do you think Octavia and Mr. Farrington are holding up?" Didi finally asked.

"Have you noticed that Octavia is hitting the bottle a lot?" Dodo responded.

"You know, I didn't like to say anything, but I have smelled it on her more than a few times this weekend." Didi came to sit by her sister on the bed. "I had no idea she was a lush. She never used to be, did she? I wonder what happened to cause such a habit?" She reached over and grabbed a pearl necklace lying on the bedside table.

"When I was talking to Freddy at the pub, he mentioned mishandling his allowance. Perhaps it is worse than he suggested, and Octavia is worried sick about him?"

"What is it with men and wasting money?" responded Didi, holding her sister's pearls up against her frock, as if testing how they looked.

"Affluence makes people less aware of the value of money in my opinion," said Dodo sagely. "Wealthy people indulge their children which only fuels the problem. There has always been money so there always will be, sort of thinking."

"Do you think we were spoiled?" asked her sister, finally replacing the pearls.

"Of course we were!" Dodo replied. "We have no idea what it's like to go without. Even during the war, we had plenty."

"Yes, I suppose you are right."

***

Marcus, Julian and Charlie had all headed for home before breakfast, after giving the chief inspector their home addresses. Julian had said an unexpectedly quick goodbye, causing Dodo to believe that the murder had interrupted any attachment he may have felt for her. She was surprised to realize that she was not as disappointed as she might have expected herself to be.

They had all three left in Charlie's motorcar and as Dodo had waved them goodbye, she had been engulfed in a shroud of sadness. It was very possible that one of them was a murderer. A chill settled over her and she hurried inside.

As she and Didi headed down to lunch later that day, they could hear raised voices coming from the library. She nodded to Didi and they knocked loudly, pushing on the door and entering. The scene they encountered was one of abject anguish—Octavia's face a mass of lines and tears and Mr. Farrington holding a letter, his expression dark.

"I'm so sorry to interrupt…" began Dodo as she and her sister turned to exit.

"Oh, Richard, shouldn't we tell someone?" Octavia's voice was woeful, and Dodo felt a flood of sympathy.

"I suppose with everything else that's happened it's likely to be discovered," he said, flatly. "Come in."

The two sisters approached in nervous anticipation. Richard Farrington stepped forward and handed Dodo the letter.

I know what you have done. You are disgusting. How will the community see you when they know?

The letters had been crudely cut from newspapers and magazines and pasted on the sheet.

"Do you know to what this refers?" asked Dodo.

"Yes," sighed Mr. Farrington. "While I was a young soldier in India, I was accused of disorderly conduct by a young woman there—"

"But he was exonerated!" cried Octavia.

"Unfortunately, it is not always the verdict of innocence that counts, but the seriousness of the charge," continued Mr. Farrington. "I was convicted in the court of public opinion, and my father made arrangements for me to be brought home. Unfortunately, my departure fueled the gossips' tongues. They used it to stoke the fire of rumor asking why I needed to slink away if I was innocent. You cannot win, it seems." He stroked his chin. "It was all years ago. Octavia knows, of course—we have no secrets—and then several months ago these letters started showing up. They badly unsettled Octavia's nerves."

Hence the drinking. "Do you have any idea who it might be?" Dodo asked.

"None whatsoever!" Richard Farrington strode about the room, restlessly.

"Have they asked for any money?"

"No, oddly," Richard said, pausing.

"But Richard is thinking of standing for parliament," said Octavia, quietly.

"Really?" Dodo looked from one Farrington to the other, her brows raised. "I had no idea you were interested in politics."

"Yes. For some years I have felt that I should like to give back, you know, and then the country seems to be headed in a direction that I do not feel is in its best interests. I thought I would throw my hat in the ring."

"Have you told anyone else about your aspirations?"

"No!" He paused. "Well, I may have mentioned it at my club in passing."

"Have you mentioned it to the police?" asked Didi.

"Goodness, no!" cried Octavia. "Then it would become public and absolutely ruin his chances."

The sisters shared a look. "Don't you think, given the circumstances, that you ought to now?" said Dodo, carefully. "They are bound to find out, and it will look bad for you."

Octavia exhaled a huge, emotion-laden sigh and Mr. Farrington gripped his mouth with his hand. "They do have a point, Tavie."

"For all his faults, I am sure the chief inspector would be terribly discreet," added Dodo.

Mr. Farrington stared at the ceiling. "I suppose you are right," he said in defeat. "Though, I don't see that it has anything to do with this case."

"Why don't you let the chief inspector decide that?" said Dodo. "One never knows how the jigsaw pieces will fit together."

"Won't it look like we have a motive?" asked Octavia in a tiny voice.

"Do you have any reason to believe the letters came from Agnes?" Dodo asked, crossing the room to sit by Octavia.

"No, but—"

"And did you kill her?" she persisted.

"No!" they both cried together.

"Then I think you have to trust that the truth will clear you both. And if they can help you find the poison-pen writer, you may be able to save your chance at becoming an MP!"

Chapter 16

"There is a telephone call for you, Lady Dorothea," announced the butler, as Dodo was polishing off some toast, dripping with jam and butter.

She nodded while licking her fingers and quickly wiped them on a serviette. She pushed her chair out, swept from the room in her freshly laundered white muslin trousers, throwing a scarlet scarf back over her shoulder.

Entering the small telephone cabinet in the grand foyer she picked up the smooth, ivory earpiece that rested on the occasional table and lifted the sleek, receiver to her mouth. "Hello, Lady Dorothea Dorchester speaking."

"Yes, Lady Dorothea," said a familiar voice, "this is Miss Grey, the librarian."

"Oh, yes! Do you have some news for me?"

"I do indeed. Shall I tell you over the telephone, or would you like to come and see it?"

"I think I'll pop down and see it. Thanks awfully! I'll be there in just a jiffy."

She ran back to the breakfast room, opened the door a crack, and caught Didi's eye, tipping her head back to indicate that Didi should leave the room.

"What's up?" asked Didi, as she entered the hall.

"The library called. They've found something. Want to come?"

The weather was fine, so they left immediately, crunching down the gravel drive in the breezy sunshine.

Upon meeting Miss Grey, Didi could hardly suppress a giggle over the woman's dowdy appearance, except that a warning look from Dodo kept her in check.

"Ah, Lady Dorothea. The assistant from the Sudbury library found some relevant newspaper articles and sent some duplicate copies for you to read." She handed Dodo a manila folder.

"Thank you so much!" Dodo flashed the broad smile she usually reserved for the chief inspector or a surly butler.

The two sisters moved to a desk with some privacy, and Dodo placed the folder on the table. They both stared at it.

"Aren't you going to open it?" asked Didi.

"Gosh, I'm suddenly nervous," replied Dodo. "I'm afraid of finding out something horrible about Julian. I was really beginning to like him."

"Well, you've gone this far! Open it up!"

Dodo opened the folder slowly and several articles of newsprint were revealed. The top one was dated just over six months before.

Headline: Local Girl Found Dead by Roadside. Her stomach dropped. "Golly, I don't think I can read the rest. Would you do it?" She was disappointed in her own cowardice.

Didi took the article and began to read. "Norma Steadman, aged nineteen, was found dead along Horsetail Lane, Thursday morning by a paper boy. After cycling to fetch the police, it was determined that the girl had been struck by a vehicle and left to die. Leaving the scene of an accident with injury is a criminal offense. Anyone with information should contact police at 50391."

Dodo's jaw dropped. *Please let this be a horrible coincidence.*

Didi raised her head, eyes wide, sucking in her lips. "You don't think that Julian…?"

Dodo took a deep cleansing breath, told herself to buck up, and grabbed the next article. This one had a picture of a young girl, full of promise, radiating a sunny light. Dodo felt sick, as though a hundred flies were raging inside her.

"Norma Steadman, aged nineteen, was killed in an automobile-pedestrian accident, as she walked home from her job as a barmaid, late Wednesday evening. She is described by locals as a lovely girl who had ambitions to become a secretary. She was engaged to be married to Robert 'Bob' Green in June.

"Friends said she walked home along Horse Tail Lane after her shift at the pub most nights. The community is reeling from the accident that took one so young and vibrant before her time. No witnesses have come forward and police are hoping that someone may have seen something that will lead to the arrest of the hit and run driver."

A macabre silence filled the space between them.

"You look rather pale, Dodo," said Didi.

"I feel ghastly," replied Dodo. "What if the driver *was* Julian? How could he slink away after doing something so awful?"

"We don't know that it was him," Didi reminded her. "All we know is that a girl was killed by a car six months ago and you have a suspicion that it might have been Julian on the flimsy fact that he pales when car accidents are mentioned. It's hardly proof positive."

"You're right. I suppose the next thing we must do is tell Chief Inspector Blood and let him do some police legwork."

"What does the last article say?" asked Didi.

Dodo moved the papers aside and slipped out the last one. It was an obituary for the poor girl. At the bottom it said, *The driver of the vehicle that killed Miss Steadman has still not been identified.*

They gathered up the papers into the manila folder and Didi put them under her arm. As they exited the library the sun was still shining brightly, but a dark cloud had settled over Dodo making the day feel gray. She spoke little on the walk back, and Didi seemed to feel obliged to keep up a constant patter of conversation about nothing. Dodo tuned her out.

As they approached the house, the chief inspector's car could be seen parked in the front. Dodo put her head down and increased her pace, causing Didi, who was several inches shorter, to trot to keep up.

Dodo pushed the door open with vigor and listened for the chief inspector's voice from the vestibule.

A rumble from the library indicated his location and she strode to the door and knocked.

"Come in!" he commanded.

They both entered and saw that Inspector Hornby and the chief inspector were making some kind of timeline about the crimes. A photograph of Agnes caught at Dodo's sympathies.

The two men looked up. Dodo noticed a softening of the hard line the chief inspector had taken with her up to now. Her bravado vanished and she slumped her shoulders.

"We have some news for you," she said, nodding for Didi to give the inspector the folder.

"News?"

"Nothing conclusive, you understand, but there was a fatal car accident six months ago in the area where Mr. Jeffries resides that left a young girl dead."

The chief inspector fingered the articles in the folder, skimming them quickly. "Good work Lady Dorothea," he said. "I will contact the local force up there and point them in the right direction."

Dodo felt anything but good.

"Oh, and thank you for encouraging the Farringtons to tell me about the poison-pen letters."

This last piece of news added even more weight to her dark mood. Everything she was discovering led to increasingly damning revelations concerning her friends.

Didi tugged her sleeve. "Let's go and find Tavie."

***

They found Octavia lounging by the fishpond feeding the koi. A white sun hat shaded her face so that when she turned, Dodo was shocked by the dark shadows under her eyes.

"How are you holding up, Tavie?" asked Didi.

"Oh, my dears, it is simply ghastly! Ghastly! We just told the chief inspector about the letters and I am exhausted. He does not think they came from Agnes as he doubts that she would have knowledge of Richard's history, but he is searching her room again. Do you know I think I'm done having weekend parties!"

"Oh, surely not!" cried Didi, dragging a white iron chair next to Octavia and taking her hand. "Your parties are legendary!"

"Well, this one certainly will be!" Octavia gasped, throwing herself back against the chaise.

"People won't hold you responsible," said Dodo.

"Won't they?" Tavie replied. "There are such snarky snobs around, you know, who live for this kind of scandal. I daren't show my face in town for a while."

"Well, who needs them anyway?" remarked Didi. "Situations like this show who your real friends are. *We* won't desert you!"

Octavia sighed. "Has the chief inspector told you *anything*?" she asked as though she was fearful of the answer. "He seems to be playing his cards pretty close to his chest."

"Not much," admitted Dodo. "Though they are following several lines of inquiry. By the way, what do you know about Anita sneaking off at all hours?"

"Sneaking off? Anita? I haven't the faintest."

"Apparently she keeps sloping off when she thinks no one is looking. You must have noticed how often she looks at her watch?"

"Yes, I did. I thought it was rather rude, you know. But slipping away. I don't know anything about that. Is she a suspect?"

"Well, it is odd behavior, and in a situation like this, it's a bit of a red flag. Could she be meeting someone who is a murderer? Is she giving the jewels to a fence?"

"Oh, yes I see. But I've known her all her life. I just can't see her doing anything nefarious."

"I believe the police are putting a tail on her," confided Dodo. *Oops, and she had promised not to say anything.*

"A what?" exclaimed Octavia, scrunching her nose in concentration as though she was trying to imagine a policeman attaching a donkey's tail to Anita's dress like in the children's party game.

"Not an actual tail," giggled Didi. "It's how the police say they are following someone suspicious. And we were not supposed to tell you -" She threw an accusatory look at her sister. "- so, don't tell anyone, or we shall get in trouble."

"Good grief! What an odd phrase."

"I suppose it is," Dodo laughed.

"Oh, my dears, it is so good to laugh," said Octavia, throwing her head back. "Though, I do feel rather guilty having any fun with that poor girl lying dead. I'm so relieved the chief inspector told her parents. I'm just not up to it, but I suppose they will come by soon for the inquest. It's such a dreadful business!"

"Is there anything *we* can do for you?" asked Dodo.

"No—yes! Could you take the poor dog for a run? He's been rather neglected with all this going on."

"Of course, we'd love to," said Dodo.

***

"Where on earth has he got to?" muttered Dodo as she walked ahead of her sister. She had thrown a raggedy old tennis ball for the dog to retrieve, which it had done several times, but *this* time the dog had not returned.

"He's probably chasing a rabbit," said Didi. "He'll come back soon enough."

They had walked away from the main gardens and into the wooded area Dodo could see from her window, which transitioned into a dense copse. The light here was quite dim due to the heavy canopy of trees. Dodo pulled her scarf from around her neck, putting it around her shoulders against the chill.

"Major!" cried Didi. "Major, come here boy!"

They trudged on toward the area Didi had thrown the ball.

"I would have changed my shoes if I had known we would be hiking!" snorted Dodo. "This undergrowth is going to ruin these—"

"There you are!" interrupted Didi. "What *are* you doing?" The dog had a hold of something between his teeth and was pulling with a vengeance. The sisters' arrival did nothing to dissuade him.

"Let's have a look at what you found," said Didi, kneeling next to Major. "Why! It's an old iron ring pull. I think it's attached to something."

Dodo, curiosity piqued, crouched beside her sister, and while the dog pulled, she brushed away some leaves revealing an old trap door.

"Well, that's interesting!" she declared. "Help me pull it open."

They nudged the dog aside, distracting him with a treat and began to pull on the ring. It was heavy but it moved up quite easily, as though it had been used more recently than one might think. The door itself was heavy and they both strained to open the thing all the way.

Dodo leaned forward to peer into the gaping hole, managing to make out some crude steps. She gingerly placed her designer shoe on the first ledge to test its integrity. She could feel that it was hewn out of rock—old and rough but sturdy.

"Up for an adventure?" she asked Didi who was standing, mouth agape.

"Rather!" she declared.

They inched down into the inky darkness and it soon became apparent that they would need a flashlight. Didi volunteered to run back to the house while Dodo waited by the trap door with the dog.

As she waited, Dodo pondered over the possibilities. Where did this lead? Was it a tunnel? Could it possibly lead to the house? How could this discovery impact the case?

She looked back through the trees. It wasn't too far from where they had played croquet. Only one person had admitted going back to the house, but anyone could have sneaked over here, if they knew about the tunnel and it did, in fact, lead to the house. It had obviously been opened quite recently, since the foliage on the top would have been much thicker if it had lain undisturbed. Someone definitely knew about it.

Gasping breaths foretold the arrival of Didi. She had managed to scrounge up two flashlights.

"Golly, I am out of shape!" She panted, pressing her palm to her chest as she sucked in great gulps of air.

"I'll go first," said Dodo. There was no rail to hold onto as they plunged back into the darkness. She switched on the flashlight, illuminating each step of the stairs as she carefully placed her foot. A smell of damp earth wafted toward her, but it was not unpleasant. Without warning, the dog pushed past her, apparently unwilling to be left out of the adventure, almost knocking her off her balance. She grabbed at the wall, brushing a root that she grabbed to keep upright.

At the bottom of the steps, the beam of light revealed a narrow passage, with rough walls covered in moss. The floor was packed dirt and mercifully had few potholes. She picked her way along, Didi following in her wake. The dog had gone on ahead, unhindered by the dark.

"It's quite spooky down here, isn't it?" commented Didi, a hint of anxiety in her voice.

"It makes me think of those old, silent horror films set in haunted houses," replied Dodo. "I keep expecting Frankenstein to materialize!"

"I think Major would warn us of any danger," said Didi.

"You're right! What a good thing he decided to join us!"

They made slow progress but after less than five minutes the floor started to rise. Major had retraced his steps and met them, tongue lolling out of the side of his mouth.

"Hello, boy! We must be close to the end," Dodo remarked.

"Thank goodness for that! I'm beginning to feel a little claustrophobic," admitted Didi.

The glow of her light showed a matching set of stairs and she shone the light up to the top. Another trap door faced her.

"I hope you're feeling strong," she said to Didi. "We'll have to push against gravity."

They stood together on the steps, switched off their lights, and raised their arms to push. Nothing happened.

"I'm going to go up a couple of steps and brace my back against the door. On the count of three, you push up with all your might," she instructed her sister.

Major sat patiently at the bottom of the steps.

"One, two, three!"

Chapter 17

Crash! An object fell above them as they heaved the door, but no light broke through the darkness as the wooden door cracked open. The weight of it necessitated that they both keep pushing until, at last, it tipped over.

They climbed out and turned on the flashlights to find themselves in a dank cellar. A tea chest had fallen over, revealing artifacts of china wrapped in newspaper. Dodo turned her flashlight to the floor around the chest.

"See these marks? Someone dragged that chest to hide this door," she declared. "And I think it's safe to conclude that a woman could not maneuver that door alone." Dodo brushed down her linen trousers that now bore brown stains and bits of dirt. Didi shook her head, earth and leaves flying off like swing chairs on a carnival ride.

"Uggh! These trousers are ruined!" Dodo complained, positioning the light on her legs to survey the damage.

"But it's all in a good cause, Dodo."

"Yes, I suppose so. We've proven that there's a means of entering the house through a secret passageway. And that it would not have been hard for someone to slip away unnoticed. Who would know about it? Freddy almost certainly, Octavia and Mr. Farrington, probably. I suppose Freddy could have shown it to his friends when they were boys. You agree with me that a woman could not manage that door alone?"

"Absolutely! Even the other door needed two of us."

"So that rules out Anita, us, Octavia, and Mrs. Alexander."

"It seems terribly disloyal, but Octavia could have managed it with her husband, as could Mrs. Alexander," Didi pointed out.

"Accomplices! Yes, good point. But two people disappearing would have been more noticeable—and Mr. Farrington was in the village according to several witnesses."

A whining from the dog caught their attention. They shone their lights up and saw him waiting at the door to the cellar.

"Come on! Let's go and find the chief inspector!"

As they emerged into the daylight of the main floor of the house, they both let out a giggle at the bedraggled state of the other. They looked as though they had been dragged through the proverbial hedge backward.

Rather than freshening up, which was a true sacrifice for Dodo, they went in search of the chief inspector and barged in on him in the library, still conferring with Inspector Hornby. He looked irritated at the interruption until he saw the two disheveled women.

"What on earth happened to you two!" declared Inspector Hornby, laughing.

Didi blushed but Dodo held her head high. "We have made an important discovery relevant to the case."

"Okay. Let's hear it!" said the chief inspector.

They related their recent exploits to the two policemen in great detail.

"Well, well! Please take us to see it," said Chief Inspector Blood.

They retraced their steps to the cellar and showed the men the gaping hole in the floor, pointing out the scrapes that demonstrated that someone had deliberately hidden the trapdoor.

"May I use your flashlight, Lady Dorothea?" asked the chief inspector.

"Certainly." She held it out, but not quite far enough, with an enigmatic smile. They locked eyes as the chief inspector closed the distance to take the light.

With flashlight in hand the two men descended. Dodo glanced at Didi as they telepathically agreed that they would follow them.

The trek back along the secret passageway to the woods seemed much shorter and they all emerged into the copse in a few minutes.

"Congratulations!" said the chief inspector. "This certainly put things in a new light. Anyone could have entered the house using this passage."

"Not anyone, Chief Inspector. It took both of us to open the trap doors. I believe that eliminates the two of us and Anita," said Dodo.

"We thought that the older ladies could have done it with their husbands," suggested Didi.

"One person slipping off might not be observed…" began Inspector Hornby.

"…but two would have been noticed," finished Dodo.

"And Dodo reminded me that Mr. Farrington has an alibi," added Didi.

"So that leaves us with the young men," said the chief inspector. "Charlie, Freddy, Marcus, and Julian. I think it is time we talked to them again. Well done ladies!"

They both curtsied.

***

Freddy sat stiff, his face blank and unemotional. Dodo found his attitude odd. "Yes, I had forgotten about it," he said in a monotone. "It was a great adventure when I was a boy, but I haven't been down there in years."

"Would Mr. Makepeace, Mr. Chadwick, or Mr. Jeffries know about it?" asked the chief inspector, looking down at his notes, not at Freddy.

Freddy looked around the room before answering. "I didn't meet Julian until I was up at college, but I probably showed it to Marcus and Charlie during school holidays." A light went on in his eyes. "It was such a spooky place—we loved to hate it. Just the thing for schoolboys in search of fun, you know."

The chief inspector scribbled away.

"In fact, I thought it was sealed up," continued Freddy. "You can ask my parents, but I thought they sealed it some years ago."

"I will do that, sir. Thank you."

The two inspectors left, and Dodo moved closer to Freddy, whose expression had taken on the blank look again.

"Are you alright? You look peaky."

"I'm fine. I'm just worried about Ma. She doesn't deal well with this kind of thing."

"I could lie and say I hadn't noticed but…"

"Father and I are worried about how much she drinks. I think she uses it as a means to escape harsh realities. I blame myself."

"Why? What have *you* done?"

"Nothing in particular," he said, pinching a piece of lint off his trousers. "I just think I'm a disappointment. I didn't finish at Cambridge, you know."

"No, I didn't," replied Dodo. "What happened?"

"It's those darned theses. I just wasn't up to the job. I missed the deadline and they failed me. Crushed my parents. It's almost impossible to get a good job without a degree these days. One can no longer rely on the family name alone, it appears." His shoulders sagged in defeat and Dodo realized that the happy-go-lucky persona he portrayed was a shallow façade that took a great deal of energy to maintain. She felt unaccountably sorry for him.

"I have a suspicion that they threw this party as a way to cheer me up," he said. "It back-fired terribly."

***

The chief inspector had been gone for most of the next day and had been unavailable by telephone. Dodo and Didi tried to find diversion where they could.

Things looked up when Lizzie came up to dress them for dinner, all of a dither.

"I have some news m'lady," she began, clasping and unclasping her hands in front of her. "I have discovered a connection between Mr. Makepeace and Agnes."

"Go on," said Dodo, sitting on the bed.

"Agnes' sister came to collect her things, and the housekeeper invited her to take tea with us. She started to cry, and Mrs. McCreedy comforted her with a hug and then the girl asked if we thought it was the cheating gentleman that did it. 'The who?' asked Mrs. McCreedy, and then it all came out.

"Agnes has a cousin who is a porter at Cambridge, and he heard the scuttlebutt that Mr. Makepeace had been thrown out for cheating on his exams. It was all hushed up, of course, since he is from such a distinguished family and all. But the sister said that

Agnes was very interested given that Mr. Makepeace was coming here for the weekend and told her sister that she was going to make some money on that information. Then she made her sister swear not to tell her family. Poor thing. She's been holding all that guilt in and it just spilled out."

"The stockings!" cried Dodo. "I had discovered about the cheating, Lizzie, but I could not connect Marcus to Agnes. Well done! You have provided the missing piece." Lizzie blushed.

When the chief inspector finally arrived, Dodo accosted him.

"We have further information that is relevant," she said directly.

The chief inspector looked around the vestibule putting his finger to his lips and indicated for Dodo to follow him.

Once they were behind the closed door of the library Chief Inspector Blood said, "Alright, Lady Dorothea. Let's hear it."

"My maid has uncovered a connection between Agnes and Marcus," she declared.

"Out with it then," he said, pulling out the notebook.

In spite of his rough manner, Dodo told him all she had learned. The chief inspector looked suitably impressed.

"Well, well, well," said the chief inspector.

"How does this sit with what you have learned?" she asked.

"Mr. Makepeace claimed he had forgotten all about the passageway but remembered seeing it as a young boy. His recollection confirmed that Mr. Farrington showed it to friends when he was younger. But we already know that Mr. Makepeace returned to the house across the gardens from his own testimony. No need for the tunnel. That alone makes him our top suspect, and now that you have linked him with the maid, well, I think we have enough evidence to make an arrest. In addition, I confronted him with the facts of his dismissal from college and he did not deny it and now, thanks to you, we know that he was the person Agnes was blackmailing. I really should contact Hornby right away." He stood to leave.

"Did anyone else know about the tunnel?" she asked, before he could go.

"Yes, Mr. Chadwick remembered the secret tunnel immediately. He said that he and Freddy used it regularly when he visited. Though he denied using it recently."

"I suppose this puts Charlie and Freddy on your suspect list too," said Dodo.

"I can confirm that these three are the focus of our inquiries, yes, but this new information seems to point firmly to Mr. Makepeace. Means, motive, opportunity."

Dodo agreed but was unsettled.

"This does suggest that the theft was an unrelated crime, does it not chief inspector?" He nodded. "Any luck on the hit and run?" Dodo continued.

"We are attempting to secure the necessary warrants to look into the residences of both Mr. Jeffries and his parents, but we are in need of more cause than we have at the present—though our constables are, at this very moment, questioning those in the pub showing a photograph of Mr. Jeffries to see if anyone recollects him being present that night."

Dodo's head ached. "I feel rather dirty learning all this," she murmured.

"You are welcome to withdraw from the investigation if it is offending your sensibilities, m'lady." Something in his tone made her look up at him, but he presented a perfect poker face.

"No, no," she replied. "It's just that it's disturbing to learn that people you respect may not be all that they seem."

"During the course of an inquiry it is not unusual to come upon other crimes or misdemeanors, Lady Dorothea. People are flawed. It is the human condition."

"Yes, yes I suppose so." She sighed.

"And speaking of misdemeanors…" Dodo's head snapped up. "I have some news about Miss Anita Anderson."

Dodo gave the chief inspector her full attention.

"It's not what you think. She is seeing a young man, not of her class."

"*That's* why she's sneaking about?"

"Yes. One of the local policemen followed her last night. She met up with the fellow in a secluded location and then my man, in plain clothes, followed him after they parted. He struck up a conversation with the chap and he, not knowing that he was speaking to a policeman, mentioned that his girl was a 'toff' and that her parents would fly off the handle if they knew, so they had to meet in secret."

"That does explain things then," said Dodo. "What a dark horse she is! Clash of the classes. Do you think those barriers will ever come down, Chief Inspector?"

His face clouded. "I think the Great War began the process but there is still a long way to go, Lady Dorothea. Let's hope it doesn't take another war to complete the process."

He put his hat back on his head and reached for the door handle. "By the way, though it seems insignificant now, I can tell you that Freddy did go to the dentist. Hornby went to see him, and the dentist confirmed that he had fixed a broken tooth the morning of the croquet game."

"Could he tell how long the tooth had been chipped?" she asked.

"No. It was impossible to tell."

"May I ask what your interest in that is?" she asked.

"I can't rightly say," he said. "It just keeps nagging at me—as though it is important, and I just can't see why. However, I can leave that line of inquiry now that you have found Marcus' connection to the maid. Right then, if you'll excuse me, I must make plans for the arrest of Mr. Makepeace." He gave a slight bow and touched his hand to his hat. "I'm indebted to you for your help, Lady Dorothea. I've been under some pressure to make progress in the case and now, thanks to you, I have."

Chapter 18

"Marcus? Arrested? Surely not!" cried Didi when Dodo informed her.

"He had opportunity, means, and now motive."

"Gosh!" said Didi. "I can't stand the man, but I can't see him murdering the girl." She threw off her shoes and lay back on Dodo's bed. "He doesn't have the gumption."

"The case against him may be circumstantial, but it's solid," Dodo pointed out. "I don't think the police have a choice but to arrest him. He was seen going back to the house around the time of the murder and the victim was blackmailing him about the cheating scandal. Any jury would convict him. But I have to admit something is bothering me. It doesn't feel right—and it doesn't resolve the theft."

"Well, there are three, maybe four, main suspects," began Didi. "Marcus, who was being blackmailed by the victim, Charlie who knew about the tunnel but seems to have no connection to the dead maid, though he does have a gambling secret, and Freddy, who obviously knows the girl, has used the tunnel, but seems to have no motive, and finally Julian. I think he should still be included because he may have fatally struck a young woman with a car six months ago and might do anything to keep it secret."

"Of those four, if it has to be one of them, I'd rather it was Marcus," declared Dodo. "Though, that sounds rather mean. At the same time, I would hate for there to be a miscarriage of justice," she continued. "Let's reconsider the croquet game to see if we can think of any discrepancies."

"I make the worst witness," remarked Didi. "If only one knew how important attention to detail would be later, one would pay more attention!"

"Too true, Didi," Dodo agreed. "But I think if we carefully reflect, we might say something that jogs our memory. Now, close your eyes and replay it all in your mind."

"The arrival was staggered, I remember," Didi began. "Octavia was out there first, making sure everything was set up.

Mr. Farrington was not there—Octavia told us one of his clubs was being mended."

"And that alibi has been corroborated," said Dodo.

"Next out was Julian. He got there before us. He was eager to see you I think."

"Mmmm. That's right. He asked to be my partner before any of the others came out. Because of my stupid infatuation with him, I didn't pay nearly enough attention to anyone else." The near constant dread crept out from the dark recesses of Dodo's mind as she thought about Julian.

"Then Anita sauntered out. I remember she had dark circles under her eyes. I almost suggested that she borrow some of my make-up but thought better of it."

"Well, that's one mystery solved," said Dodo. "She seems so strait-laced, but it would explain her lack of interest in the chaps here for the weekend."

"I can't believe what the chief inspector told you," said Didi. "Would *you* have a relationship with a working-class man?"

"I don't honestly know. Here I am thinking I'm so progressive and modern and find I am quite shocked by Anita's behavior. We don't really know our own prejudices until we are smack up against them. In theory I am for the idea, but in practice…"

"I know exactly what you mean," said her sister. "The war did break down class barriers to some extent but certainly not all the way. I wonder if the time will come when it really will not matter what class people are from—that marriages across classes will be the norm?"

"I cannot imagine such a time, I must say," mused Dodo.

"Could you visualize having a relationship with Inspector Hornby for example?" Didi pushed. "He is very good-looking."

"There's more to relationships than looks though, Didi. We would not have anything in common. And the chief inspector clearly has a chip on his shoulder as regards the upper classes."

"The chief inspector? I don't like him very much. He rather frightens me—he's so gruff. Hornby is much more approachable. Can you imagine taking in a show with him?"

"I can't honestly say..." she trailed off, looking out the window but not seeing anything.

"Okay, back to our suspects," said Didi. "Freddy, Charlie and Marcus came out together about five minutes later," Didi continued with her eyes shut tight, "and lastly, the Alexanders. I remember that I asked to take their picture. Oh, my goodness, Dodo! I completely forgot that. I had my *camera* with me, and I took some pictures during the course of the game. The Alexanders were less than enthusiastic as they were still smarting from the theft, so I left them alone, and decided to just take candid pictures of the rest of us."

"Good girl! Where's your camera now?" asked Dodo.

"In my room." Didi jumped up and disappeared into the adjoining room. When she returned, she was swinging her Brownie camera from its leather strap.

"We need to get that film developed," said Dodo. "It might have some clues on it!"

***

The photograph developer had said it would take a few hours to develop the film. In the meantime, they called the chief inspector from the public phone box.

"Chief Inspector Blood?" said Dodo after they were connected.

"Lady Dorothea, what can I do for you? I'm very busy right at the moment." He sounded distracted. Time to re-focus his attention.

"We have made another important discovery." Aim and fire.

The tone of the chief inspector's voice sharpened satisfactorily. "You have?"

"Yes! We were making our own timeline of the afternoon in question and Didi suddenly remembered that she had taken some photographs with her camera. It has been so ghastly since the murder, that she completely forgot all about it. We have just dropped off the film for developing."

"I'm sorry, Lady Dorothea, I'm just not seeing why this is important. We have our man in custody."

"Don't you see?" Dodo ploughed on undaunted. "We are hoping that the pictures might hold some clues as to who was where and when. If someone used the tunnel and they are not in the pictures it might indicate who. It will help cement some of the alibis."

"You make a good point, but it hardly seems relevant now."

"I know the evidence against Marcus seems overwhelming, but I feel…I don't know…like the puzzle isn't quite finished."

"Remember, I have to go where the facts lead, Lady Dorothea. I cannot succumb to my *feelings*."

Dodo sucked in her cheeks, smarting at the insult. And just when she had started warming up to him. *Insufferable man!*

"What does Marcus say?" she retorted.

"He is proclaiming his innocence. But they all do."

"Yes, I see your point. Thank you for your time, Chief Inspector." She hung up feeling like a schoolgirl who had just been reprimanded by the headmistress.

"What did he say?" asked Didi. Dodo filled her in.

"Oh. That rather takes the wind out of our sails."

"I still believe that something on that camera may change things," said Dodo. "I can't believe I am going to bat for that boar but being a brat does not necessarily make him guilty of murder."

***

They passed the time by having tea and cakes in the village teashop, though neither one particularly enjoyed them.

As soon as the appointed hour came, they pushed through the door to the photographer's shop. Dodo could not explain the sense of urgency she felt.

"Hello again, ladies," said the developer. "I am just waiting for your prints to dry." He disappeared back into the dark room.

Dodo heard a rhythmic tapping and then realized that it was her own toe. She looked over at Didi who had an annoyed, pinched face. "Sorry," she said.

A chemical, musty smell permeated the whole room, and she scrunched up her aquiline nose. Didi seemed relaxed, perusing the prints hanging on the walls.

Why am I so anxious?

After an eternity, the door scuffed open again and the man re-appeared holding a brown paper bag. They quickly paid and ran out to the bench that sat along the side of the village pond.

As the ducks quacked pleasantly, Dodo took out the pictures. They showed small groups of people unaware that their pictures were being taken. There were shots of couples hitting the croquet balls, others of people awaiting their turn or cheering their last success.

Dodo flicked to the last one and sat back in defeat. "Drat! I'm not sure what I was hoping for, but it's not there."

Didi slipped the pile from her sister's hands and looked at the prints more slowly. Dodo closed her eyes, disappointment draping her like a cape. She let the warm sun soothe her as Didi shuffled the snapshots. Then the shuffling stopped. Dodo cocked her head and opened one eye. "What?"

"I think I found it…" said Didi. "But you are not going to like it."

Chapter 19

"What am I looking at?" Dodo queried.

"Look for something that is in one of the photos but not in the others," coached Didi.

Dodo re-examined each picture carefully, trailing her gaze from one person to the next in an effort to deduce what her sister already had. She saw Freddy and Anita watching Marcus hit the ball successfully through a hoop. In the next picture Freddy was swinging the mallet at the ball. He was wearing sunglasses. She quickly dealt through all the rest of the pictures. He was only wearing sunglasses in the one picture.

"Do you remember what order these were taken in?" asked Dodo, her pulse ticking up. Didi took the prints and laid them out on the bench in order. The picture with Freddy wearing sunglasses was the second to last picture of the day. The very last picture was of Octavia right before the alert that the murder had occurred.

"What do you think it means?" said Didi, cautiously.

"I think it means that Freddy went back to the house during the game, unnoticed, and unconsciously picked up a pair of sunglasses on the way out," she said. "And now we know how he could do that without being seen. This is extremely incriminating, but what possible motive could he have?"

"It's time to start a search for one," replied Didi. "Of the four suspects, he has been considered the least likely and so has had the least research time spent upon him. We should probably tell the chief inspector."

Dodo felt the now familiar twist of her stomach. Could her childhood friend really be a murderer? "Chief Inspector Blood was rather rude to me when I just called," she said. "He thinks he has his man. Perhaps we should investigate ourselves and only alert him if we find something."

***

"So, Freddy chipped his tooth?" stated Dodo after finding Octavia reclining by the pond again. She had begun a conversation about the weather and the dog and casually inserted this comment into the middle of it.

"Yes, I believe so," Octavia drawled. Dodo looked at the empty glass on the little side table.

"How annoying? I had a chipped tooth once and it made my tongue awfully sore. I had to get it seen to immediately."

"Yes, I had a crown fall off a year ago. It was very uncomfortable," Octavia agreed.

"The sooner these things are seen to the better, I think. When did Freddy chip his?" She was going for a nonchalant tone but still held her breath.

"Let me see," said Octavia, picking up the empty glass and tipping it to her lips. "Wednesday was it? No, not Wednesday. Thursday. Yes, Thursday. No. Wait. Couldn't have been Thursday, that's the day you all arrived. Must have been Friday."

Dodo made an effort not to roll her eyes with exasperation. "Friday then? That makes sense since he got it seen to Saturday morning. It would have bothered him if he'd left it." Why then had Freddy gone to great lengths to tell them he had chipped it earlier in the week?

"Quite right! Dr Meadows is a friend and he went in specially to see to it on Saturday. So nice of him."

"Yes, it was," said Dodo thoughtfully. "I've got a bit of a toothache myself. Do you think he would be able to see me on short notice?"

"Darling! Just mention my name and he'll get you in lickety-split."

***

"What seems to be the problem," Dr. Meadows asked as he dragged the overhead light over to look into Dodo's mouth.

Pointing to a molar, Dodo said, "This one has been giving me problems on and off. Just want to check that I don't need a filling." The dentist picked up a tool and poked at the offending tooth. He drew her lip down and prodded around the gum line. "No decay," he concluded. "I suggest you change your toothpaste. I have some samples in the front office. The tooth looks fine."

"Thank you *so* much for seeing me," she gushed, turning on the full power of her smile. "Freddy told me how good you are and that you had come in on your day off to help him in his time of need."

"Known the family a long time," he said. "They pay on time, unlike so many, and I am happy to accommodate them."

"When did Freddy say that he had chipped the tooth?" she asked.

"Just the night before, it had already rubbed his tongue raw," the dentist replied.

"Thanks again," she said, sliding off the dentist's chair and heading toward the receptionist.

"Think nothing of it," said the dentist, already looking at the notes for the next patient.

Why had Freddy lied and what was the significance? Time to poke the bear.

***

"Lovely man, your dentist," said Dodo at dinner that night. Freddy stopped cutting his meat and looked up with surprise.

"How on earth would you know?" he asked, caution vibrating in his tone.

"I had a bit of a toothache, so I went to see him," she replied.

"Oh," he said, going back to carving his steak.

"He told me how sore your tongue was because of the chip," she continued.

"Yes, it really was," Freddy replied.

"He mentioned that you chipped it on Friday," she ventured, looking down at her plate. In her peripheral sight she noticed the cutting stop, abruptly.

"No," said Freddy firmly, waving his knife in the air, "he is mistaken. I broke it on Tuesday." The knife hung, suspended in motion, waiting for her to agree.

"Silly me. I must have got the day wrong. Did Didi mention that we plan to play tennis tomorrow?"

She looked up at him with a disarming grin.

Freddy slowly dropped the knife and wiped his mouth with a napkin. "No, she didn't. I can't make it tomorrow." He placed the knife and fork neatly on the plate, pushed his chair back, and placed the napkin by the side of the plate. "Please excuse me, Mother. I'm feeling a little under the weather."

"Of course, dear," Octavia muttered as he left the room.

Dodo stared at the half-eaten meal with a sense of foreboding.

***

Dodo spent a restless night and as soon as was polite the next morning, she walked down to the village to use the telephone box. She had decided that to use the telephone in the house would be unwise.

A woman and her child were already in the booth when she arrived, and she had to wait. The child, a skinny boy wearing his school uniform, stuck his tongue out at her through the glass and pulled his ears. She mimicked the action eliciting a toothy smile from the freckled boy. He pulled at his mother's sleeve to have her look, but Dodo quickly stopped the childish taunt.

The woman seemed to take forever, and by the time she finally replaced the receiver, Dodo had become very anxious. Multiple grocery bags were lifted from the floor and the young mother, with the child and the bags, squeezed out of the tiny booth. Dodo nodded politely and then hurried in.

She placed the coins into the slots and waited for the operator.

"Where shall I direct the call?" said a peppy voice.

"Chelsea 324 please," replied Dodo. She heard some pips and then the operator said, "You are through."

"Hello, David Newman please," she said.

"Whom may I say is calling?" replied a nasally, high-pitched voice.

"Lady Dorothea Dorchester." She found her full name opened doors when necessary.

"I'll put you through," said the receptionist.

"Dodo! It's been an age!" The familiar booming voice of David Newman, stockbroker, brought a smile to her face. "What can I do for you?"

"It is in your professional capacity that I need some information," she said.

"Interested in a little speculation?" he asked.

"No." She laughed. "I am following a hunch about something and wondered if you could put your ear to the ground."

"I always have my ear to the ground, darling. In the world of finance, it is essential to know what is going on."

Dodo explained what she wanted him to find out.

"Hmmm. As long as I don't run into that pesky confidentiality thing, I think I can help you—even if it's at the local pub. May I ask why?"

"Sorry. Having confidentiality problems myself, but if my hunch is correct you will hear all about it soon enough."

"The plot thickens!" David chuckled.

"I know. I apologize for the cloak and dagger but if you could help me, I'd be very grateful."

"Grateful enough to accompany me to my cousin's wedding?"

"Absolutely! Let me know the details and I'd be happy to go with you."

"It's a date, then!"

"Yes! And David, thank you."

"Of course."

She replaced the receiver, her hand lingering, and tarried in the box. She had now set things inexorably in motion and there was no going back.

Walking quickly back to the house, she hoped that her early absence had not been noticed, thus avoiding having to lie about where she had been.

As her shoes crunched up the gravel drive toward the front door, she thought she heard something and hesitated, turning to see if she could hear from which direction the noise had come. She took a step back and as she did, she heard a rush of air and a great, ground-shaking thud just behind her. Turning in shock she saw that it was a huge stone urn.

Hand on her hat, she looked up at the roof to see if someone had pushed it but seeing no one she fled into the house and raced up the stairs to her sister's room.

"We need to go up to the roof. I think someone just tried to kill me!" she gasped.

Didi jumped up and they mounted the servant's stairs to the roof. As they entered it was clear that gravel was scattered on the flat part and she hurried to the side of the roof straight above the front door. An urn was clearly missing—the stains from years of rain around the bottom of the urn had caused a ring on the stone. Upon inspection Dodo could see footsteps in the gravel near where the urn had been.

"Look, someone has been up here and pushed the urn that used to stand here," she explained.

Didi looked over the parapet and witnessed the upturned urn on the driveway in front of the house. She turned, hand to her chest, face pale.

"Is Freddy home?" Dodo demanded.

"Freddy? No. He left early this morning to go into town. You don't think him capable of something like this?" she asked in alarm.

Dodo removed her hat and leaned against a wall. "I'm not sure what to think at this point," she said with exasperation. "All my friends seem to have skeletons in their closets. I'm beginning to feel that I don't really know any of them."

"Freddy would never hurt you," protested Didi.

"When someone is trapped in a corner and the prospect of hanging is in the picture, I think that anyone might be capable of anything to avoid the noose," she responded.

Chapter 20

They both flew back down the stairs to see who was in the house and found Octavia in the drawing room asleep. Didi roused her by shaking.

"What on earth…" slurred Octavia.

"Someone just pushed an urn onto Dodo!"

Octavia looked at Dodo, puzzled. "She looks fine to me," she said.

"They missed," said Dodo tartly.

Octavia looked at her clasped hands. "I'm sure it was an accident, my dear. I think you must be seeing crimes everywhere. We are all a little on edge."

"I don't see how it could be an accident," Dodo pursued. "It was far too heavy to have been moved by the wind. Who else is here?"

"Anita just left. She forgot something when she went home and came to get it, and of course Richard. You are overwrought, Dorothea. Perhaps you should have a lie down."

"I think it is time we left," rebutted Dodo.

"Really?" Octavia seemed genuinely upset…or was it relieved? "If you think that's best darling. I want to thank you so much for staying on to help me at this trying time. Will you at least stay for dinner?"

"No," said Dodo decidedly. "I think I'd like to get home before dark." She grabbed Octavia's hands and planted a perfunctory kiss on her cheek. Didi followed suit. Dodo noticed that Octavia sunk back onto the settee as they left.

They called for Lizzie and she came up to help them pack.

"May I ask why you are leaving so suddenly, m'lady?" she asked.

The two sisters exchanged a glance. "Were there any visitors today, Lizzie?" asked Dodo.

"Miss Anita was here for a bit, but I didn't see anyone else."

"Someone pushed an urn from the roof onto Dodo," declared Didi.

Lizzie's hand flew to her mouth. "No!" Her eyes were wild.

"Yes!" said Didi with emphasis.

"We feel it is a good time to leave. I can continue my sleuthing from afar. You can come in the car with us this time."

"But who would do such a thing and why?" asked Lizzie as she pulled a suitcase out from under the bed.

"I must have touched a nerve with some of my inquiries," mused Dodo.

"Are you going to tell the chief inspector?" said Didi, opening the dresser drawers and throwing items to Lizzie.

"No! He is not in my good books at the moment. Such a tiresome man."

"Is Marcus still in jail?" asked Didi.

"I suppose he must be," she replied. But he could not have pushed the urn.

"Oh yes," interrupted Lizzie. "The butler read about his arrest in the newspaper. Shocking it is."

"We don't think he committed the murder," said Didi. "And if he is currently in custody, he could not have done this to Dodo."

"Really?" said Lizzie pausing as she smoothed another dress to fold and put in the trunk. "Who do you think it was, then?"

"The jury is still out on that," explained Dodo, imperceptibly shaking her head at her sister, "but we have various tentacles of investigation."

Lizzie frowned, her maid's headband low on her brow. "And you think the guilty party might have tried to put a stop to your inquiries?" she asked.

"I don't know what to think, but it does look that way which narrows the field a great deal if no one was in the house but the Farringtons and Anita!"

They finished up the packing and hurried out to the garage where the Farrington's chauffeur jumped up in some state of dishabille. "M'lady, I was not expecting anyone or I'd have—"

"Don't worry yourself, Mr. Parker. This is a sudden change of plans," explained Dodo.

"I have your keys right here, Lady Dorothea, if you'll just hang on a jiffy." He entered the office and came back holding keys with the solid silver 'D' keyring, then set about fastening their luggage to the back of the Bentley.

"You are a dear," said Didi, batting her eyelashes at the young man who blushed to the roots of his red hair.

"Just… doing… my job, m'lady," he stuttered.

They clambered in and Parker turned the starter for them. Dodo put the car in gear with only a little grinding and they backed out, waving madly at the chauffeur who stood bemused, looking as though he was not sure if it was his place to wave back.

As they raced out of the gates, they almost collided with Freddy, who laid on his horn before he saw who the culprit was, then flung his hands in the air. Dodo threw her head back laughing a little hysterically and flooring the accelerator of the powerful, sleek car.

It felt good to be leaving.

***

"What is all this about Marcus Makepeace being arrested for murder?" shrieked Lady Guinevere Dorchester as they entered the dining room. The candles on the table threw a warm, comforting glow around the space.

"I was hoping you hadn't heard," sighed Dodo. They had arrived home just in time for dinner.

"Not heard? It's all over town!" continued Lady Guinevere. "Why do they think it was Marcus, for goodness sake?"

"Unfortunately, Mummy, the evidence the police have so far points straight to him," said Didi. "Did you know he cheated on his exams at university?"

"Well, I can't say that surprises me, but it will come as a terrible shock to his parents."

"Not as much as being arrested for murder." said Dodo, wryly.

Her mother put a handkerchief to her mouth. "Yes, you do have a point there. But how could the cheating be connected to that poor girl's murder?"

"Marcus was unlucky enough that a porter at the college is a cousin to Agnes Brown, the maid who was murdered, and he told them all about it at a family dinner. Well, when Agnes heard that he was going to be a guest at Farrington Hall, she thought it might be a chance to make some real money by blackmailing him. She was the type apparently. He did, in fact, give her some money. She used it to buy expensive silk stockings. The police believe that Marcus panicked when she demanded more money and killed her on the spur of the moment."

"And he was the only one that admitted to returning to the house before the murder was discovered," added Didi.

Lady Dorchester's hanky moved down to her throat, and she sucked in her cheeks. "Oh yes, that is rather damning."

"If it's any consolation, Dodo and I do not believe he is the murderer," said Didi.

Her mother's brow rose.

"He is surely guilty of being an oaf," continued Dodo. "But we have uncovered some evidence that incriminates other people."

Didi waved her hand. "Yes and…"

Dodo shook her head violently at her sister who frowned, then seeming to realize her error continued "…oh, and the stubborn chief inspector from Scotland Yard isn't listening because he thinks he has his man." Dodo sighed in relief that she had managed to stop Didi telling their mother about her narrow escape.

Didi threw her an apologetic smile.

"What kind of evidence? Perhaps your father can talk sense into this inspector."

"If you are upset that they think it might be Marcus, consider the other people in the party, Mother. All the 'best' kind of people. If it's not him, it must be one of them. It's a daunting thought."

"Yes, I see," agreed Lady Guinevere. "Terrible business! What is the world coming to? I must write to Ariadne Makepeace and offer my support," she declared.

"Sorry about that," said Didi after her mother was well out of earshot, "I wasn't thinking. Of course, we shouldn't tell Mummy about the urn. She would worry terribly."

"She would likely forbid us to continue our sleuthing and probably send us to India or something!"

The door to the dining room swung open revealing the butler. "Ahem," he began, "there is a phone call for Lady Dorothea." His nose began to rise and his eyes close as he waited for her to react.

"Thank you, Cartwright." She rose and left the room, heart thudding uncomfortably in her chest.

She opened the door of the little telephone cupboard, closing it firmly and reached for the receiver, sucking in a deep breath for courage. "Hello, Dorothea Dorchester speaking."

"Lady Dorothea? Chief Inspector Blood here," came the voice at the other end. Her shoulders relaxed.

"Oh, Chief Inspector! What can I do for you?"

"I thought you would be interested to know that we have conducted a search of Mr. Jeffries parents' home and my men found a car, parked in his parent's garage, covered with a dust sheet, hidden behind some packing cases."

"Oh!" said Dodo, sinking onto the little chair in the telephone closet.

"The car has a large dent in the front and though someone has tried to clean it, my men found a trace of blood on the fender. Though certainly not conclusive, it does appear to have been in an accident involving a victim. As you know, we are continuing our inquiries by questioning those in the pub that night and showing around a picture of Mr. Jeffries. No luck as yet, but if we find a witness, the dented car will become pretty damning evidence."

"I was so hoping to be wrong," said Dodo, tracing her finger slowly along the glass of the telephone cabinet, "but in my heart I think I knew. Thank you for telling me Chief Inspector."

"If knowledge of this had come to Agnes, it would give Mr. Jeffries a motive for the murder, but he does not appear to have had the opportunity, therefore I am still confident that we have the guilty party in custody. However, if we succeed in finding a witness putting Mr. Jeffries at the pub that night, he will be arrested for manslaughter and leaving the scene of an accident, at the very least."

Dodo's insides twisted fiercely but she made a decision. "About the murder, Chief Inspector," she started. "I know you did not put any stock in my sister's photographs, but we did find something ... incriminating." There was a pause at the other end and Dodo waited.

"Go on." He sighed.

"Freddy was not wearing sunglasses that day until right before the murder was discovered. He did not have any in his pocket or around his neck before that. He *must* have gone back to the house."

"The photographs show this?"

"Yes. Didi took many candid shots during the game and she noticed that in the shot she took right before the hue and cry, Freddy was wearing black sunglasses. We searched the other pictures and there was no evidence that he had any with him, Chief Inspector. And remember, he denied going back to the house, but he knew about the secret passageway better than anyone."

Silence.

"What motive would he have?" the chief inspector eventually said. "Mr. Makepeace has a strong motive, and I like him for the crime."

"I know that we have not uncovered a motive thus far, but are you aware that someone attempted to kill me today back at Farrington Hall?"

"Are you alright...? I mean, no, no I had not heard that. Did you contact the local police?"

"Oh, you *do* care! And I thought nothing could penetrate that gruff persona! I am fine, thank you, and no, I did not contact the police as I was fearful for my safety and just wanted to get away as quickly as possible, but I am telling you now."

"Please tell me exactly what happened, Lady Dorothea."

Dodo detailed her brush with death.

"And only the Farringtons and Anita were in the house?"

"Yes, but if you were trying to kill someone, you wouldn't announce your presence. It might be worth checking everyone's whereabouts, Chief Inspector."

"You make a valid point, Lady Dorothea. I will do that immediately."

"There is one person it could not have been," she continued.

"Marcus Makepeace," said the chief inspector, his voice dropping with the realization.

"Yes! It couldn't have been Marcus as you have him in custody!"

Another deep sigh passed down the telephone line. "This puts a spanner in the works," said the chief inspector.

"Isn't it just as valuable to eliminate people from an inquiry as to find evidence against them?" she asked.

"Yes, I suppose so. I shall have to let him go…let's go back to Freddy's sunglasses," he continued, his tone more subdued.

"Freddy denied going back to the house, but the photograph shows that he must have gone back during the game. He would have inadvertently grabbed the sunglasses as he left. The fact that no one noticed him leave strongly suggests that he used the tunnel. The question is, if he is innocent of the murder why the need to lie about returning to the house?"

"If he killed the maid, we need to find out his connection to her. Any ideas, Lady Dorothea?"

"Actually, I do. I've asked a friend to look into it. I thought this phone call was my friend calling me back. I'll let you know if he turns up anything."

"Very good," said the chief inspector.

"There's more," she added. "I paid a visit to the Farrington's dentist. Freddy chipped his tooth on Friday not Tuesday as he said. He lied about that as well."

"Did he now? I'm still not seeing the significance of the difference in the timeline, but it certainly calls into question everything Freddy has told me." He paused. "I trust I will see you at the inquest?"

"Indeed, you shall, Chief Inspector! We've been called as witnesses. There was a telegram waiting when we got home. I assume all the guests have received the same summons."

"I'm sure they have. Goodbye then, Lady Dorothea. I shall see you at the inquest. And take care of yourself!"

***

A couple of days later the headline in *The Times* screamed, *Son of Earl released from jail after new evidence exonerates!*

"Well!" expostulated Lord Dorchester. "Is this your doing?" he pointed his breakfast fork at Dodo.

"Guilty!" she declared with a half grin.

"He is innocent I assume?" He peered at her over his half-moon spectacles, bushy eyebrows jumping around.

"I would not call Marcus Makepeace an innocent, Daddy, but he is not guilty of *this* crime."

"Meaning?"

"He sat in the car while Didi and I tried to change a tire in the rain!"

"Ah, yes. I can see him doing that."

"And he *did* cheat on his exams at college," added Didi.

"Not cricket that! Shameful!" commented their father. "Do the police have another suspect in mind for the murder of that poor girl?"

The two sisters exchanged a look. Dodo had brought Didi up to speed on all the latest developments. When she answered her father, Dodo was cagey. "Possibly. I believe they are widening their investigations in the wake of Marcus's release."

Fortunately, their father had already found another article that caught his attention and was now engaged in the black and white print.

A slight ringing could be heard and several minutes later the butler arrived and in his deferential tone announced, "The telephone for Lady Dorothea."

"Dorothea Dorchester," she said into the ivory mouthpiece.

"Dodo! Good! Look you were right."

"David! What have you found?"

"Remember that scandal last year in the US called the Teapot Dome Scandal?"

"You mean the bribery and oil scandal?"

"Yes! Well, a lot of British investors tried to get in on the action with the Mammoth Oil Company. It was touted as a sure thing. Then the US Congress smelled corruption and after an investigation the Supreme Court withdrew the drilling rights. A lot of people lost a lot of money. Guess who is listed as an investor?"

***

Being right was overrated.

Dodo replaced the receiver long after David Newman had hung up. Life was so much simpler when one was a child. The bombshell that David had just dropped on her was going to change lives, and those people would probably blame her for uncovering it all—though logic told her that it would all be discovered at some point anyway. *And* a girl had lost her life, she reminded herself.

She sighed deeply, gathered up her courage and picked up the receiver again. "Scotland Yard, Chief Inspector Blood, please."

Chapter 21

At Chief Inspector Blood's request, the players in the drama had reluctantly gathered, once again, at Farrington Hall. The inquest into the death of Agnes Brown was to be held that afternoon, and they had all been summoned as witnesses to attend. The chief inspector had used the occasion to assemble the suspects in his inquiry beforehand. One did not turn down such an invitation.

Dodo had dressed conservatively as suited the circumstances, in a charcoal gray skirt, short-sleeved, palest pink cashmere sweater and a silk scarf. She had felt depressed since the house of cards had crashed and was having trouble maintaining her poker face. Dash it all! These were people she cared for!

After the revelation from Dodo concerning the failed oil investment in the US, the chief inspector had galvanized his men to perform a thorough fiscal hunt, and she knew that while they were all gathered here, a covert physical hunt was being conducted to recover one emerald necklace.

They were now all convened in the drawing room. Dodo glanced around the room, avoiding eye-contact with everyone except Didi. Octavia Farrington, usually the life and soul of any party, was subdued though alert and kept touching the bottom of her hair. Mr. Farrington's complexion was flushed. The Alexanders were clutching each other's hands. Three of the young men were sitting on the same side of the room, but no one was talking. Only Anita and Marcus seemed relaxed. Anita was leaning back in her chair examining her vibrant nails, and the recently released Marcus had the confidence of exoneration.

Chief Inspector Blood cleared his throat, and everyone gave him their full attention.

"First of all, I would like to thank everyone for coming this morning. I am sure you are all anxious to know who murdered the maid, Agnes Brown and who stole Mrs. Alexander's emeralds." Nervous glances bounced around the room like ping pong balls.

"However, before we get to that, I would just like to acknowledge the help of Lady Dorothea Dorchester, who has been an invaluable asset in my investigations." The chief inspector nodded in her direction, and she bobbed her head in acceptance of the compliment though she took no pleasure in it. Her detecting had unintentionally thrown a noose around one of her friend's necks and uncovered countless other weaknesses.

The chief inspector had previously asked her if she would like to be the narrator for the denouement, but she had refused. Though such an offer had elevated him in her estimation.

"We now know that Agnes Brown was an unscrupulous, ambitious, reckless girl who had ideas above her station," he began. "Living amongst the wealthy had given her a taste for the finer things in life. These characteristics would unfortunately lead to her untimely death." Octavia Farrington nodded mournfully.

"When I was first brought in on the case, I could not assume that the two cases, the theft and the murder, were connected.

"As you all know, our attention immediately turned to Mr. Marcus Makepeace as a suspect in the murder, since a witness testified that Mr. Makepeace went back to the house before the murder was discovered, a fact he initially denied. When confronted with the witness statement, he admitted to returning, but adamantly denied murdering the girl.

"As the only person to admit to opportunity, we were obligated to investigate further."

Marcus pulled his cuffs down and smoothed his hair, calm in the knowledge that he had been released from prison and was no longer a suspect, Dorothea supposed.

"Lady Dorothea called some mutual friends and made the interesting discovery that young Mr. Makepeace was under investigation at Cambridge for cheating on his exams and had been quietly expelled.

"When Agnes' sister came to collect her belongings, she disclosed that their cousin was a porter at the college Mr. Makepeace had attended and boasted of the scandal at a family dinner. Such a situation, if it became public knowledge, would bring disgrace on the Makepeace family who have been alumni at

Cambridge for generations. Agnes must have recognized the name from the guest list that had been posted in the kitchen at Farrington Hall and an idea began to form.

"Lady Dorothea had noticed that Agnes was wearing silk stockings when she died, not something a maid would normally be able to afford. This hinted at blackmail. We guessed she would have blackmailed the jewel thief. At the time of the murder, we were unaware of Mr. Makepeace's troubles and thus had no reason to connect him to the silk stockings. However, when Agnes' sister came, she was distraught and asked if the man who had paid for her sister's silence had killed her."

"Upon further questioning, the sister reported that Agnes had sworn her to secrecy but told her that she was going to approach the man who had cheated and make some money.

Now we were getting somewhere. Marcus Makepeace had opportunity, means, and now, a motive. We could do nothing less than arrest him."

Dodo looked over at Marcus and saw that the tips of his ears had turned red. He looked steadfastly at his shoes. Though he annoyed her, she sympathized with him. He may have been exonerated of the crime of murder, but he had disappointed his family and would not be accepted into any other British university.

"In fact, with the arrest of Mr. Makepeace, I became convinced that the two crimes were separate—since the motive for the murder seemed to be to stop the blackmail about the cheating scandal.

Of course, when crimes continued after his arrest, crimes which led to his release…"

The people in the room stirred, some of them clearly having no idea what the chief inspector was talking about. Dodo scoured the faces in the room.

"I had to go back to square one and reconsider all the facts with a different eye." With perfect timing, he walked to the other side of the room. Every pair of eyes followed him.

"This time, I reviewed the evidence with the mindset that the thief and the murderer were one and the same person."

A slight murmur bubbled around the room. Dodo wondered what was going on behind the expressions she could see.

"I imagined that Agnes Brown had somehow witnessed the theft," he continued. "We know that she was an opportunist who was already extorting one of the guests. She would have had no compunction about blackmailing someone else. She appears to have realized that she had been presented with a way to make a great deal of money—even speaking of leaving service and hiring her own maid. Little did she imagine that a thief might murder when backed into a corner."

The room was now so quiet that Dodo could hear the ticking of the little carriage clock on the other side of the room.

"Given the amount of money we found among her things," the chief inspector continued, "we ruled out the staff as suspects as it was unlikely that they would have such means at their disposal.

"We focused our attention on the family and guests."

A few people shifted in their seats. Dodo felt the tension rising.

"After reviewing notes from our initial interviews, it became clear that almost everyone had an opportunity to steal the jewels. Mrs. Alexander had not taken the precaution of putting them in her safe that day and anyone could have gone into her room and found them."

Anne Alexander sniffed into her handkerchief.

"On the other hand, the opportunity to commit the murder was not so universal as Agnes was seen alive before the game by the kitchen staff. Therefore, only someone going back to the house during the croquet game would have been able to kill her. Mr. Makepeace was the sole person who admitted to returning and he had already been removed from the suspect list. I had hit a wall."

Anita sneezed pulling everyone's attention to her. "Sorry," she muttered.

The chief inspector continued. "Death by strangulation does not require super strength when carried out with a scarf therefore the method of death did not rule out a woman. That left us with eleven potential suspects who all had the means, as the scarf appeared to have been dropped on the landing, but none of whom appeared to have the opportunity. That is a big pool of people." He cleared his throat.

"And then there was the problem of motive. Who would need to steal the jewels that set this whole tragedy in motion?"

Dodo thought about the things she had learned about the people in the room. Most of them had reason to be tempted by those jewels.

"Ruling out the Alexanders proved impossible as it was more than feasible that they had faked the theft in an attempt to claim on the insurance, though they strongly denied it. However, a little checking proved that their finances were not as robust as they had once been, and a further red flag was that the murder was carried out with Mrs. Alexanders own silk scarf." Mrs. Alexander's hand flew to her scarlet throat. Dodo tried to rustle up some sympathy but failed.

"The hosts, Mr. and Mrs. Farrington, appeared to have the least motive for the theft. Mr. Farrington recently had great success in his investments and was flush with money. Why would they need to steal the jewels?"

Mr. Farrington scratched his nose. "Did he have his own suspicions?" Dodo wondered.

"However, during the course of the investigation, it was revealed that someone had been intimidating Mr. Farrington on a personal matter. Could it have been Agnes?" All eyes slid to Mr. Farrington who went scarlet, dropping his eyes to the ground. "But an iron proof alibi placing Mr. Farrington in the village eliminated him." Dodo appreciated that the chief inspector did not betray the confidence he had promised the Farringtons.

Richard Farrington wiped his brow.

"Now to Mrs. Farrington. She was a great admirer of jewelry and admitted to coveting the beautiful necklace, in public. Was the envy enough to push her to theft?"

Octavia Farrington, incensed, went to stand but her husband pulled her down and rubbed her hand tenderly.

The chief inspector continued, "Again, we could find no evidence of this and as the hostess of the croquet game she had no occasion to return to the house. With no opportunity to commit the crime, we moved on."

Octavia's eyes fill with unshed tears. Dodo's heart squeezed in her chest.

"Diantha and Dorothea Dorchester appeared to have little need for money or jewels and we could find no secret need for quick cash. Though, we did check their finances and their rooms. If they were not the thieves, then they would not be the subjects of the blackmail and so we eliminated them from our inquiries." This was news to Dodo but she was not surprised. It was standard procedure.

Didi uncrossed her legs and slipped to the edge of her seat, hands folded, waiting. Dodo had not told her about her latest discovery.

"We turned our attentions to Mr. Charlie Chadwick, man about town and jovial houseguest. He swore that he had not returned to the house during the croquet match, but an eyewitness saw him come into the kitchen around the time of the murder."

What? The chief inspector had not shared this information with Dodo. Her gaze cut over to Charlie who had paled.

"He had persuaded a maid to fetch him some brandy as he said he was in need of something stronger than the lemonade that had been provided. Not a theft worthy of prosecution, though in poor taste, but this did give him the opportunity to murder the maid if he was the jewel thief. Did he have a motive for the theft? A little bird suggested that we check with a certain bookie in Southwark who revealed that Mr. Chadwick was in serious debt after losing on too many horses. The said bookie, a felon well-known to the Yard, was threatening violence. Thus, Mr. Chadwick became suspect number one."

"I say! I'm a bad gambler but I'm not a murderer!" cried Charlie.

"I agree," said the chief inspector matter-of-factly.

"Oh!" said Charlie, the air punched out of him.

"Though you were in desperate need of funds to stay the bookie, when we went back to re-interview the maid, she swore that you did not leave the kitchen that afternoon and further testified that she saw you hurry back to the game long before the alarm went up about the murder." Charlie straightened his cravat, nodding.

The chief inspector resumed his narrative. "During our preliminary interviews, a suspicious piece of news concerning

Miss Anita Anderson had reached our ears." Anita's head snapped up, and her gaze swung wildly around the room.

"She had been seen stealing away from the house after dark during the weekend. What would necessitate such conduct in a well-to-do young woman? Such a risk to her reputation was worth investigating. Was she perhaps fencing stolen goods?"

Anita's eyes widened with fear.

"One of my plain clothes officers followed Miss Anderson on one of her jaunts and witnessed a rendezvous with a young man."

At this point Anita blushed to her roots and bit her nails. Was he really going to embarrass her?

"The officer withdrew to give them some privacy but after the encounter, he followed the young man and struck up a conversation. He learned that the gentleman was a working man who had begun a liaison with a young woman of class which necessitated them meeting in secret. This seemed to answer the question about the need to sneak around. If other leads failed, we would return to this young man and search his home and question his associates."

Chief Inspector Blood stopped in his narrative and glanced at Miss Anderson who was exhibiting every sign of embarrassment. She could not stop fiddling with the buttons on her cardigan.

"We met about six months ago," she said quietly, head down. "He is exciting and not at all like my own set. It's been rather thrilling as the whole thing is clandestine and we meet when we can. My parents, obviously, would not approve." She looked up anxiously. "You won't need to tell them, will you?" she asked the chief inspector.

"I don't see why," he replied.

Octavia looked as though she had accidentally bitten into a lemon and Dodo felt the untimely urge to laugh.

"In the meantime, we began investigating Mr. Julian Jeffries." The chief inspector paused. "You do not drive a car Mr. Jeffries, isn't that true?" Julian's face fell, and he shifted his shoulders. "No," he replied, "but what has that got to do with anything?"

Dodo's heart sighed. She knew where this was headed, and she wished she could vanish. If the crime Julian had committed had been less serious she would have felt a twinge of guilt at being the source of the chief inspector's inquiries. But she did not.

"Is there a reason for that?" pushed the chief inspector.

Julian looked up glumly. "I suppose you already know why," he mumbled. The young, debonair beau seemed to shrink before Dodo's eyes, melting into the sofa.

"Yes, but I'd like to hear it from you."

"No, no," Julian whispered. "You have the floor."

"If you insist." The chief inspector straightened his tie and Dodo held her breath. "I heard it mentioned that you did not drive, which I thought odd for a young man of your station. One of the great things about my position at Scotland Yard is that I have many resources available to me, and I had some of my people research the local newspapers from the area where you live, from the last twelve months." He sent a quick look to Dodo who breathed out in relief that he had not mentioned her as the resource.

"They found an article about an unsolved hit and run that killed a young bar maid." Julian could not look up. "Following a hunch, we showed your picture around the pub where she worked and asked if you had been there the night of the accident. Several people remembered seeing you that night and that you'd had a little too much to drink. This was enough to secure a search warrant for your home and your parents' home. It will come as no surprise to you that in your parents' garage, we found a car, shrouded with a dust cover, that showed evidence of extensive damage. Why have you never taken it to a body shop, Mr. Jeffries? Was it so that no one would report the damage that would connect you to the crime?"

Julian raised his head in wretched agony, his eyes shadowed with grief. In spite of everything, Dodo pitied him.

"It was dark, and I had stayed too long and drunk too much," he groaned. "I swear I did not see her until it was too late. She must have been walking in the middle of the dark road. I jumped out of the car after the impact and ran to give her assistance if I could, but it was clear that she was already gone. I panicked, and seeing no one on the road, drove home and hid the car. It has haunted me ever since. I suppose you will have to arrest me?"

Dodo stared at him, willing him to look at her but he would not.

The chief inspector nodded.

"It's actually quite a relief," Julian sighed. "Such guilt is a heavy burden. I regret it very much." He finally flung an apologetic look at Dodo.

She smiled weakly back.

"Perhaps you also killed the maid because she learned of your misdeeds and threatened to expose you? We know she was an accomplished blackmailer," continued the chief inspector. *What was he playing at?*

Julian jumped up. "I swear I did not," he moaned. "No one has put the pieces together until today. My secret was safe, I was only threatened by my own conscience."

"Yes," agreed the chief inspector. "A terrible secret but not, I have come to believe, the one that got Agnes killed."

Julian slumped back down in his seat looking ten years older.

"The only person who seemed to have no motive and no opportunity was young Mr. Farrington," picked up the chief inspector. "This piqued my curiosity. Then by sheer chance, Lady Dorothea and her sister discovered a secret passage leading from the copse to the basement of the house. A tunnel with trap doors so heavy that a young woman alone would not have been able to open them. This eliminated the young ladies as suspects."

Didi smiled at Dodo.

"Now, of the young men, who would know this tunnel better than the one who had lived all his life in this house?"

There was a rustling as everyone sat up. A secret passage.

"Through this tunnel, Mr. Freddy Farrington would have been able to enter the house without being seen and, if he hurried, no one would even notice he was missing from the group.

"I was also interested in the fact that young Mr. Farrington had chipped his tooth some days before. This information would not stop bothering me. Did it have any bearing on the case? An idea tickled the edge of my mind, but I could not, at first, see its relevance.

"Then Lady Dorothea took it upon herself to go and see the dentist and learned that Freddy had lied about *when* he had chipped the tooth." Dorothea shifted in her seat. "Now why would he need to do that?" The chief inspector asked the room. "It was not earlier in the week as he had told everyone, in fact, it was the very day of the theft. The light of understanding began to dawn."

It was Freddy's turn to look at the floor.

"From years of solving crimes I knew that many women who own expensive jewelry have imitation jewels made that they take when they travel, often at the behest of their insurance companies. Someone who had a little knowledge of jewels and who would only have been interested in the genuine article, would have had to test the emeralds for authenticity and what better way than biting into them. Such a test might chip a tooth if the jewels were real, might it not Mr. Farrington?" The chief inspector was now staring straight at Freddy whose face was ashen.

"Following this line of reasoning I theorized that Agnes may have seen Freddy biting into something in Mrs. Alexander's room and then, after hearing the report that the necklace had been stolen, even she would have easily put the pieces together. She had already succeeded in getting enough money to buy silk nylons out of one victim. She would not have been able to pass up an opportunity to make even more money. She worked for the family and knew that they were very wealthy. However, she appears to have miscalculated as for some reason Freddy must have refused to pay and Agnes pressed the matter by threatening to expose him as the thief. Is that how it went Freddy?"

Dodo cut her glance to Octavia who had her knuckles to her mouth.

"It's like you said. A theory. Fiction. You have absolutely no evidence," retorted Freddy. "Why would I possibly need to steal anything?"

"You are correct. As yet I have laid out no evidence. Let me continue."

Octavia was clasping a handkerchief to her throat, her eyes haunted and desperate.

"As Mr. Freddy Farrington has just pointed out, there were still pieces of the puzzle missing. We could find no motive for the theft and although we had found the secret passage, we had no proof that Mr. Freddy had used it to enter the house that day.

"Then fate handed us a break that I at first dismissed, but which cracked the case wide open. Lady Diantha had a camera with her on that fateful day. In the commotion, she had forgotten all about it. A few days later, her memory was jogged, and she remembered that she had taken candid pictures throughout the afternoon until the murder was discovered."

A subtle shift fell over the room.

"She went to the village to get the film developed, and there lay the clue to the whole case." Chief Inspector Blood held some snapshots aloft. "In the early pictures Freddy is not wearing sunglasses and they are not visible anywhere on his person but in the last picture before the murder was discovered, he is. *He had to have gone into the house during the game and accidentally picked up the glasses as he left.*"

All eyes in the room were now on Freddy.

"We now had means, and opportunity. It was time to look for a motive. Up to then we had not concentrated any effort on Freddy as there were so many more likely suspects.

"At first I was reluctant to utilize Lady Dorothea's help in this case. I am not accustomed to civilians interfering in police business, but my boss impressed upon me the fact that Lady Dorothea's connections in the world of the aristocracy and her previous history with crime solving would be an asset. He was right.

"Lady Dorothea set about investigating recent troubles in the financial world through her contacts and soon hit upon a jackpot. The American Teapot Dome Scandal, which was widely reported on in the British press, had also claimed many British investors as its victims. Listed among those victims was one Frederick Farrington. We finally had our motive."

A sharp cry attracted the attention of everyone in the room as Octavia clutched at her heart.

Chapter 22

"Get her some water!" commanded Mr. Farrington as Octavia slumped against the edge of the sofa. A maid was called and dispatched as Mr. Farrington tried to give aid to his distressed wife. He twisted in his seat.

"Tell me this is not true, Freddy?" he cried.

Looking like a small boy with shoulders hunched and chin down, Freddy sat in shocked silence.

A knock on the door interrupted the unfolding drama and a constable poked his head around it, beckoning to the chief inspector. After a minute, Chief Inspector Blood returned to the center of the room holding a package.

"While we have been talking, a search of the grounds and house has been conducted. This was found hidden in a packing case in the cellar." The chief inspector opened the paper to reveal the gleaming emeralds. Anne Alexander gasped.

"I believe these belong to you," said the chief inspector, handing the necklace out to her. She took it with subdued reverence.

Dodo watched Freddy—a rangy rabbit caught in a trap. A confusion of emotions ambushed her. He turned hunted eyes on every occupant of the room, clearly thinking through his options. Eventually, seeing no way out, his shoulders slumped, and his face collapsed. "Oh Father, I have ruined everything! I thought I could prove to you that I am every bit as good a businessman as you and I speculated on those oil deposits in America that I was assured were solid. I wanted to surprise you and show that I was a chip off the old block and borrowed heavily against my inheritance.

"Then the scandal of corruption broke that went all the way up to the President of the United States, and I was left with a debt so great that I could not bring myself to confess it to you. It would have necessitated mortgaging this house and I could not face it. I was ashamed. Desperate." His voice was gaining in pitch and elevation.

"I overheard you and Mother talking about Mrs. Alexander bringing the emeralds, and I saw an answer to my problems. I knew they would be insured. No one was supposed to get hurt!" He wiped his mouth with the back of his hand, falling on his knees by his parents.

"Then, out of the blue, Agnes terrified me by sending a note saying that she knew what I had done but that she would keep quiet for a price. I panicked and arranged to meet her during the croquet game so that there would be no witnesses, to explain that I had no money to pay her. She became unreasonable and started saying terrible things. My eyes fell on the scarf that had fallen on the floor and I picked it up. She would not stop talking, and in a moment of madness I just wanted her to be quiet and I—" A sob restricted further words, and he dropped his head into his hands.

"But why did you try to kill Dodo?" demanded Didi.

Freddy lifted his tear-streaked face, his brow crinkled in confusion. "What are you talking about?" he whispered, "I would never—"

"That was me," came a strangled confession from the ailing Octavia.

"*You?*" cried Dodo feeling suddenly as though she had dropped from a great height.

"I was on the telephone with the dentist's wife about flowers for the church and she mentioned, in passing, that you had asked her husband about the day Freddy's tooth was chipped. He had found it odd and talked about it at lunch.

I realized during my police interview that there had been a moment when Freddy was not out in the garden during the game and I started putting two and two together and drew the awful conclusion that Freddy may have had something to do with the murder. I just wanted you to stop asking questions. I simply wanted to scare you. Of course, I missed on purpose, Dodo."

The sadness that had swept over Dodo was instantly banished by shock and betrayal.

Chief Inspector Blood nodded to the constable who moved forward to make the arrest.

"Don't use handcuffs!" pleaded Freddy. "I will come quietly."

The chief inspector gave his approval and Freddy stood, reaching out a hand to his mother who was completely overcome with grief. The constable forced him out the door and Octavia crumpled.

"Lady Dorothea," asked the chief inspector, "will you be pressing charges?"

Octavia's pitiful head snapped up.

Dodo blinked to clear her head. "No! No. Let's forget that ever happened, shall we?"

Octavia reached toward her, but Dodo brushed past and out of the room.

***

There was little need for the inquest now that the murderer had been apprehended, and the chief inspector asked Inspector Hornby to make sure that it was canceled.

As all the guests prepared to leave, the chief inspector sought Dodo out. For the first time, she noticed that he had replaced the dull raincoat with a tailored suit and had cut his hair. It suited him.

"Lady Dorothea—"

"Dodo," she interrupted.

"Dorothea…"

She stared up at him to see a softness that was unexpected. Sympathy she supposed.

"I would like to thank you again for your help and apologize for any dismissal you may have felt from me during this case."

Dodo kept her eyes locked on his, pursing her vermillion lips and flicking her head slightly, knowing her hair would swing and shine like tassels on a dress. The chief inspector pulled at the tie knot at his neck.

"Like I said, I appreciate that your amateur sleuthing was invaluable to the case and that your position in society enabled you to open doors that were closed to me."

Dodo bit her lip. "My position in society?"

"Your being an 'Honorable', and all that," said the chief inspector, his eyes crinkling at the corners.

"Ah, that," she commented, smoothing her skirt to give her hands something to do. "It opens doors and throws up walls, Chief Inspector. One a help, the other a hinderance. I quite admire Anita for her courage to buck the system."

The chief inspector swallowed hard, placed his hat on his head, and held out his hand. Dodo reached to shake it.

"Do you believe he will hang?" she asked.

"Freddy? It was a crime of passion, but the theft will muddy the waters. I wouldn't be surprised."

"I think it will kill his mother," she said.

"And all hopes of his father of running for parliament."

"Oh yes. I had forgotten about those ambitions." She dropped her hand. "I wish we had never come on this wretched weekend," she blurted out.

"I don't," said the chief inspector, tipping his hat and spinning away leaving Dodo aghast.

***

There were no fond farewells from the bruised participants of the house party, everyone eager to be on their way, slipping quietly out, except Julian and Freddy who had both been taken into custody.

After an hour on the road, Didi finally asked, "Why didn't you tell me everything?"

"I was sick at heart, darling." Dodo shifted into a lower gear as they glided around a country corner. "A piece of our childhood has been shattered into a million pieces never to be put together again. I couldn't bring myself to tell you."

"Did you ever suspect Freddy before we developed the photographs?"

"No. One doesn't suspect one's childhood friends of murder; people who served to add threads to the tapestry of one's idyllic childhood."

"The chief inspector clearly did. After Marcus' innocence was apparent anyway," she mused.

"Yes. Freddy appeared to be too much above the fray. That in itself was suspicious. The day I visited his dentist was the first time I really started to think Freddy might have something to do with the whole sordid mess. I went hoping to exonerate him and ended up putting the proverbial nail in his coffin."

"You brushed off Octavia well and proper," said Didi. "I still cannot believe it was her that pushed the urn. I was so convinced she was asleep when we found her, and she certainly held her nerves together."

"You don't blame me, do you?" Dodo replied. "Tavie claims she never meant to harm me, but think about it, we only have her word. I'm still smarting. The best I could do was to refuse to press charges."

"Don't blame you at all, old thing!" replied Didi. "You're a better woman than I. I think I would have slapped her at the very least."

"Oh, I wanted to!" declared Dodo. "It is all so terribly upsetting. Thankfully, I have a trip coming soon to Paris to work with Renée. Now I can't wait to get away!"

Seeing a clear stretch of road ahead, Dodo pressed down on the accelerator, breathing into the wind, relishing the breeze rushing through her hair.

More innocence lost, she thought as they drove toward the hazy horizon of the English countryside.

The End

I hope you enjoyed Book one of this cozy mystery and love Dodo as much as I do.

Interested in a free prequel to this series? Go to https://dl.bookfunnel.com/997vvive24 to download Mystery at the Derby.

Book two of the series, *Murder is Fashionable* is available for $1.99 on Amazon. https://amzn.to/2HBshwT

"Stylish Dodo Dorchester is a well-known patron of fashion. Hired by the famous Renee Dubois to support her line of French designs, she travels between Paris and London frequently. Arriving for the showing of the Spring 1923 collection, Dodo is thrust into her role as an amateur detective when one of the fashion models is murdered. Working under the radar of the French DCJP Inspector Roget, she follows clues to solve the crime. Will the murderer prove to be the man she has fallen for?"

To learn more about the series, book two and three as well as other information go to my website: www.annsuttonauthor.com

You can also follow me on Facebook at:

https://www.facebook.com/annsuttonauthor

About the Author

Agatha Christie plunged me into the fabulous world of reading when I was 10. I was never the same. I read every one of her books I could lay my hands on. Mysteries remain my favorite genre to this day - so it was only natural that I would eventually write my own.
Born and raised in England, writing fiction about my homeland keeps me connected.
After finishing my degree in French and Education and raising my family, writing has become a favorite hobby.
I hope that Dame Agatha would enjoy Dodo Dorchester at much as I do.

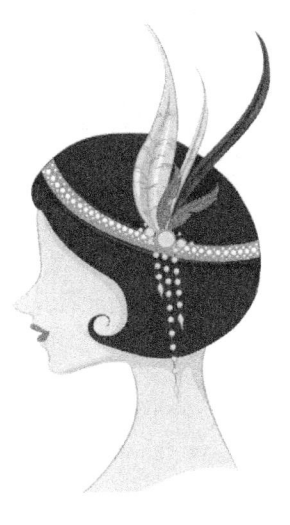

Acknowledgements

My critique partners, Laurie Snow Turner and Mary Malcarne Thomas
So many critique groups are overly critical. I have found with you guys a happy medium of encouragement, cheerleading and constructive suggestions. Thank you.
My proof-reader – Tami Stewart
The mother of a large and growing family who reads like the wind with an eagle eye. Thank you for finding little errors that have been missed.
My editor – Jolene Perry of Waypoint Author Academy
Sending my work to editors is the most terrifying part of the process for me but Jolene offers correction and constructive criticism without crushing my fragile ego.
My cheerleader, marketer and IT guy – Todd Matern
A lot of the time during the marketing side of being an author I am running around with my hair on fire. Todd is the yin to my yang. He calms me down and takes over when I am yelling at the computer.
My beta readers – Francesca Matern, Stina Van Cott, Aimy Kersey
Your reactions to my characters and plot are invaluable.
The Writing Gals for their FB author community and their YouTube tutorials
These ladies give so much of their time to teaching their Indie author followers how to succeed in this brave new publishing world. Thank you.